BLAZE OF GLORY
DARK LEOPARDS MC

LIBERTY PARKER

CONTENTS

Note to readers — iv
Acknowledgments — vi
Blurb — ix

Prologue — 1
1. Blaze — 9
2. Blaze — 19
3. Glory — 31
4. Blaze — 43
5. Glory — 53
6. Blaze — 65
7. Glory — 73
8. Blaze — 81
9. Blaze — 91
10. Blaze — 99
11. Blaze — 109
12. Blaze — 119
13. Glory — 125
14. Blaze — 133
Epilogue — 141

Liberty Parker Follow Links: — 150
Also by Liberty — 152
Co-written series — 154

COPYRIGHT

This is a work of fiction. Names, characters, places, and incidents are either the product of the author's imagination or used fictitiously, and any resemblance to actual persons, living or dead, business establishments, events or locales is entirely coincidental.

Blaze of Glory
(Originally part of the Dark Leopards MC Anthology)
Copyright 2020 © Liberty Parker
Published by: Liberty Parker
Editor: Darlene Tallman
Formatter: Liberty Parker
Cover by Tracie Douglas of Dark Water Covers

ALL RIGHTS RESERVED. This book contains material protected under International and Federal Copyright Laws and Treaties. Any unauthorized reprint or use of this material is prohibited. No part of this book may be reproduced or transmitted in any form or by any means, electronic or mechanical, including photocopying, recording, or by any information storage and retrieval system without express written permission from Liberty Parker, the author / publisher.

This was originally part of the Dark Leopards; Tall Dark and Dangerous Anthology. Kane is used with permission from Lauren Firminger and Bolt with permission from Grace Brennan. They were original characters from the West Texas anthology piece. Any use of their characters or mine without written permission and consent is punishable by law.

NOTE TO READERS

This has been changed and expanded from the first release. Most of the story is the same as it was in the Anthology, but as I went in and added here and there, I had to redo the Epilogue to complement the changes. You will notice added scenes and expanded paragraphs. Not all have changed, it is the same story, just longer than it was originally. There will be two books to accompany this piece, it's still a short story, but answers will be tied up into a pretty bow by the third book.

Have to have some suspense right?

I don't as of yet have titles to the next couple of books, but the characters will be Echo and Maritsa in one, and another will have Angela and Jake. I don't yet know which will be released next, but you will be getting both of these couple's HEA's. Until that time comes, please enjoy Blaze and Glory's story.

Love always,

Liberty

ACKNOWLEDGMENTS

I want to acknowledge Grace and Lauren for joining me in the journey of the West Texas chapter. Working with the two of you was so much fun, I hope we can do it again in the future.

To my PA Sharon Renee, thank you for always standing beside me and joining me on my next adventure. You always leap in headfirst and ask questions about my craziness later. Love you to pieces.

To all of the ladies who joined forces in the original anthology, you all will hold a special place in my heart, thank you for all of your hard work.

To my support teams; Liberty's Luscious Ladies, Twisted Iron Groupies and Rebel Guardian Insiders, without you all, none of this would be possible.

To all of my readers and supporters, I hold you all with the highest regards. Thank you for believing in me and falling in love with each character.

DEDICATION

This is dedicated to all MC and shifter lovers everywhere. Combining the two was fun and I hope you've enjoyed the journey.

DARK LEOPARDS

MOTORCYCLE CLUB
TEXAS CHAPTER

BLURB

Blaze Montgomery, the president of the West Texas chapter of the Dark Leopards MC, is up against his biggest challenge he's faced yet. Women and men are missing from his town, he's beside himself trying to figure out who they are and what they're up to. Why his town? Why his people? When he discovers the truth behind these questions, how far will he go to save them all? Betrayal unlike any he's ever come up against slams unceremoniously into him. These were trusted members of the shifter community. He believed in them and supported them, but now, what will that end up costing him?

Glory Montgomery is on a mission. As the mate and old lady to Blaze, she must overcome her personal feelings and support him no matter what. Her best friend has lost everything, and Glory must sit idly by and watch as her friend struggles through her latest tragedy... one that ends up being the club's worst nightmare come to fruition. Can she keep their secrets closely guarded? Or will she end up hurting her mate and club while caring for her friend?

As secrets unfold and life turns their world upside down, will these two mates make it through? Will they hold strong to one another and come out on the other side unscathed? Only time will tell.

Blaze of Glory

USA TODAY BESTSELLING AUTHOR
LIBERTY PARKER

PROLOGUE

BLAZE

"Son of a motherfucking bitch," I furiously hiss in despair when I see the mounds of papers spread out in front of me. Another *human* woman has been kidnapped, taken from our territory, I'm fucking livid and ready to blow some shit up. Human women have been vanishing in our town for the last six months or so, and I'm fed the fuck up with it.

We've been swarmed by the local law enforcement, begging us to assist them in this investigation. Folder after folder sits on my desk, stacked on top of one another, all containing pictures and information on what's been gathered and processed so far. The women have absolutely nothing in fucking common with one another, and I've wracked my brain trying to come up with a solution to capturing these assholes.

Yet, I have nothing to work with, no place to begin and start my search. No leads are staring me in the face; causing my skin to crawl as fur breaks out, covering my arms and hands. My leopard is angry, vengeful, ready to annihilate the threat to his brethren and town folk.

Innocents lives are being shattered, bringing out the protector side of me. I can't sit idly by and watch families being torn apart, women being stolen out of thin air. It's as if they've vanished… never to be heard from again. And that's wrong as fuck. It's this sort of situation that has had me scared witless to bring cubs into our world. People vanish without a trace, and that's a parent's worst nightmare come to fruition. I won't put my mate through that… not now, not ever.

My name is Blaze Montgomery, and I'm the president of the West Texas Chapter of the Dark Leopards Motorcycle Club. This club is my family, an indestructible brotherhood of shifters, some leopards, some not. Either way, I could care less if my brothers were purple unicorns, as long as they abide by our laws and enforce our ways.

We aren't what you'd call a lovey-dovey sort of MC, we get down and dirty. We take no prisoners, and we make no apologies for the way we live. Our existence to the humans has been a well-hidden secret for generations.

We know what could happen to our kind if we were discovered. Scientists would use us as a way to weaponize the world. Each and every shifter is unique, have their own brand of specialized gifts, some that could end world kind, and some that would always keep us ahead of the enemy. Shifters will never sit back and allow ourselves to become used in an evil capacity. We're all... one way or another, protectors... it's written in our DNA.

There are some evil shifters born, they usually turn rogue and we have to hunt them then irreverently put them down. Not something we take lightly, not something that's easily done. We weigh all of our options and try to reform them if we can. But sometimes, it's impossible to do.

When our abilities are used against, instead of for humankind, they must be put down, for the better good. It hurts my soul every time we're informed by the council that another shifter has been sent above. Some of our brethren's shifter races are dwindling; they'll be extinct soon; we need to figure out how to save their breeds.

There's been talk of starting some sort of reform sanctuary. The details are still being worked out, however, but we're supposed to be voting on it... and I'll vote *yes* as long as it's not torturing our kind in any way.

When the club was first started, you could only hold an officer's patch if you were of the leopard breed; now, we've slowly begun changing that. If you are not a leopard, you can hold an officer's patch, unless it's that of the president or vice-president. It's worked out in our favor, seeing as most of my officers are other breeds of shifters, my most entrusted group of men.

I couldn't imagine my table missing these men. The shift that has happened in our club is the best thing that could have happened in my personal opinion. It's a closely guarded secret, only being passed down to the two heads of each club.

Everyone else is left in the dark for a reason. It's not that we enjoy keeping secrets from our brothers, it's to ensure the survival of our club. We can't have a shifter war happening, we have to protect our own at whatever that cost may be. It's never to be written down or spoken of, it's an unwritten rule that death will occur if our reasons get out.

We're typically all cats of one type or another, it's the only way we could co-exist with each other. My door flies open and I see my beautiful mate, Glory, come rushing in, fear consuming her as she runs to me. My body stiffens in alertness as she makes her way to me.

"Blaze. Oh my God, Blaze," she cries out, planting her ass in my lap and her tear-stained face into my chest.

"Talk," I bark out from fear and worry.

"My friend, Angela, just called me," she sniffles.

"Your human friend from work?" I inquire.

"Yes, her daughter, Maritsa, is missing. She just vanished into thin air walking home from school today. The police aren't taking her calls of worry seriously. They say she's probably just hanging out with some friends or not wanting to come home. They won't file a missing person report for forty-eight hours… it's atrocious, Blaze. But we know that she didn't just not show up at home to hang out with friends, they had plans to go shopping for a prom dress. Maritsa has done nothing but research stores and dresses looking for the perfect one. She wouldn't miss it, it's all she's been able to talk about for the last two weeks since they began planning it. Something's terribly wrong, Blaze, I can feel it. We have to do something!" She hysterically babbles through her sobs.

All I can think about is my latest report, the one that says a young lady on her way home from a college class disappeared without a trace. The cops assumed it was the same scenario that was dished out to Angela. They can take that dirt and shovel it down their damn throats.

I'm tired of these lazy as fuck assholes who'd rather shove a donut in their mouth than do some authentic police work.

"I'll look into it," I promise her, knowing in the back of my mind that we have yet another young victim in our midst.

GLORY

I just can't believe it! Disappeared walking home from school. How does that even happen without *one* person witnessing an abduction of a young woman? No one has come forward stating they saw something; my friend is beside herself. The entire reason she called me, other than a shoulder to cry on, is because she knows my man is the president of the club.

He'd do anything for me, as I would for him. I've known Angela for going on ten years now; she's human, but she's got a heart of gold. I was instantly attached to her upon our first meeting.

We work together at the school's resource office. Angela took off early to go and prepare for a much-anticipated outing with her baby girl. Her miracle. Angela was told from an early age that conceiving would be next to impossible for her. Her fallopian tubes are riddled with scar tissue, it was only discovered when she went to seek help from the doctor for the inexplicable pain she'd suffer during her menstrual cycle.

The day my poor friend found out she was expecting, her husband was killed in a motorcycle crash on his way home from work. He passed without knowing that they'd managed to defeat the odds stacked against them. He never knew the joy of impending fatherhood.

When we speak about Calvin, it always has a tinged of sadness attached to it, even when it's a happy memory. I feel bad for Maritsa that all she knows of her father are stories from her mother and a photo album Angela put together for her. And now, Angela's possibly lost her daughter to the hands of another. We have to find Maritsa and bring her home.

As I burrow deeply into my mate's embrace, I begin to fall asleep from utter exhaustion. I feel the toll from my emotionally charged mental breakdown. My poor, poor friend. I can't even imagine how she's feeling... losing the two most important people in her life in tragic ways.

As darkness takes hold, I hear these words from Blaze. "We will find her and bring her home, love. I promise you; I will not stop until she's home."

ONE
BLAZE

I relentlessly, and tirelessly, cover all land in my territory. Each and every day I've taken it upon myself to go out and look for clues, the missing link. The women may be disappearing from my town; but they sure as fuck aren't being held here. I've left no stone unturned in my pursuit of tracking down these missing girls and women.

I've reached out to our other Texas chapters, who've all promised to keep their ears to the ground and eyes wide open to intruders in their territories. The word has gone out, I've made sure it's well-known that I am searching far and wide for these trespassers. No one will be left unpunished from the Dark Leopards MC once I get my hands on them.

My men are riled up; ready for a fight. We don't take indiscretions against women lightly. We may be a band of misfits who run drugs, weapons and a few other illegal operations, but we don't ever hurt women or innocents. We take out the trash every so often for our town's sheriff and chief of police. When their hands are legally bound, they call on us.

We have an arrangement of sorts. Chief Anderson keeps his nose and men out of our business dealings, and we keep the town in order. Bliss Creek, Texas, a place we call home, used to be a meth town, but we came in and cleaned house. Not because we give a fuck about what they do on their own time, but because this is where we're settling and choose to raise our families.

I'll be damned if that poison touches the ones I care about.

It also was due to the fact that we wanted to be the only distributors in the area. Meth, cocaine, weed; we're a one-stop shop. If you need it, we've got it. We use the cover of our chop shop, under the disguise of a legally owned junkyard. The drugs are transported inside of the used parts from vehicles in house. It's been lucrative in supporting the club. The funds alone will ensure my great-grandchildren never have to work a day in their lives. The phone rings, bringing me out of my mind's distraction.

"Hello," I pick it up and answer without looking at the caller ID.

"Blaze, we've got another one it appears. Her name is Maritsa..." I don't allow Chief Anderson to finish his sentence since I'm already aware of her status. He's the one I deal with on a case by case basis. I don't really tolerate the sheriff, he's old school and a pain in the ass. Chief Anderson knows this and always takes it upon himself to keep me in the loop and vice versa with the sheriff.

"Know this already, my old lady is friends with her mother, Angela. She's already reached out to us for assistance, seeing as one of your men informed her that it's just the wild act of a teenager. Tell me, why is it your men are sitting back and allowing her to become just another statistic?" The accusation in my voice silences him for a brief moment before he continues.

"We've kept the missing women quiet so you and your men can do your thing. I chose to keep things on the downlow so your investigation isn't interfered with." His excuses are just that... full of fucking bullshit.

"Not good enough of an excuse, Chief!" I bark into the phone. "She's a fucking teenager, goddammit! Just shy of her seventeenth birthday. At such a young age, her life will forever be changed. We need to broadcast this far and wide so that the public is keeping their eyes open and children coveted." I inhale a deep breath, trying to reign in my explosive temper.

"I'll have a media press conference later this afternoon. Is there anything I should keep quiet?" *In my pocket*, I greedily smirk at his question and my after thought.

"Keep it simple, Chief. Just announce that we have a random number of missing women from our territory. Let's ruffle some feathers and announce that we have suspicions on who they are and that the local MC is assisting in this investigation. I want to see if it causes someone to freak out and make a mistake."

"If this gets in the hands of the FBI, we're all in trouble, Blaze."

"I'll deal with that when the time comes. I've got some contacts high up that should nip that shit in the bud," I authoritatively state. Shifters are everywhere. In every office, including that of our commander in chief.

"I'll set it up to where it hits the five o'clock news," he informs me before disconnecting the call.

Now that they know they're being watched, they'll be overly cautious, which means a mistake will be made. I just need them to make one. I call Kane and inform him that things are fixing to get interesting for us. My men are knowledgeable on a brief basis, but I've kept some things close to the vest, things I know I'm gonna have to lay out the details to for them all later.

GLORY

Angela doesn't become a shell of a woman; she becomes a fighter for her daughter's cause. We've been printing out missing person flyers and hanging them in every store window, all town poles, and some have made their way onto the internet's numerous sites for missing and exploited children. The only thing that bothers me, is that we've found out that there are twelve missing women and children in our area alone.

How does this even happen without it becoming public knowledge? Why would the town bury this and not make it public knowledge? Something isn't settling right in my gut; I'm fixing to call out all of these politicians and public figures asses if something isn't done soon.

I'm on my laptop when something catches my attention. I've done a google reverse search using Maritsa's photograph and have happened upon an auction site. One very deeply embedded in the dark web. Not easily found, but it's hit on her thanks to facial recognition.

Fuck, she's being auctioned off like cattle! I have to get to Blaze and tell him immediately. I can't let Angela see this, especially seeing as Maritsa's currently being bid on. I feel like a shit friend hiding this from her, but there are words used that threaten my kind.

My shifter brethren.

This is not good. I fear for what's being done to Maritsa now and what possibly could happen if we don't find her quickly.

Young mates.

Breeders.

Those are the two key phrases that stick out like a sore, abused thumb. They are kidnapping humans in order to change them into shifters and use them for breeding purposes. Some give up waiting on their destined mates to find them, needing offspring to carry on their lineage. But this, this is going too far. It has to be stopped. I make my excuses and leave Angela, who is lost in her own world and barely acknowledges that I'm leaving.

"Blaze," I reach out using our mate link. He doesn't answer, which means he's blocked any outside interference. Looks like I'm gonna have to search him out the old-fashioned way and invade whatever it is he and the men are up to.

There are certain things, as his mate, I get away with that no one else would. Not usually interrupting their private meetings, but in this instance, I think he'll forgive me… eventually anyways.

BLAZE

We've just wrapped up church and I'm sitting in my office chair when the door bangs open. It's déjà vu when Glory comes charging in. "You have to see this," she demands as she opens up her laptop in front of me. Is that the way I'm gonna be greeted by her these days? She's on a mission it seems and has forgotten the right way to greet her mate.

"Well, hello to you too, Glory," I tease her. She gives me a no-nonsense look as she finds the page she was searching for.

"This isn't a joking matter, Blaze. Look!" My eyes follow her finger and widen when I see what she's pointing at.

"Motherfucking, son-of-a-bitch!" I roar out as I read the site's details. They're offering human women to be changed as potential, unwilling mates, and auctioned off as breeding stock to all shifters. "How did you find this?"

"Remember that program I downloaded a few years back when I was searching for my father?" I nod my head remembering her doing just that. "I did a Google picture reverse search using it, and voila!" She points to the picture of Maritsa in a cage, eyes wide and a terrified look plastered on her face. "I've heard ramblings of shifters freaking out due to their kind going extinct. I never in a million years thought they'd be taking this road."

"Desperation does crazy things to a man. I still find that I have a hard time understanding them hitting this level, however. We have to stop this. Glory, I need you to send this link to me in an email. Can you do that for me?" I'm nowhere near as technologically adept as she is, but I can click on a link and follow it.

"Yeah, do you want me to send it to Dakota as well?" Dakota is known to the brothers as Decoder, but Glory was around as he grew up and always calls him by his given name. He's a whiz on a computer and can break any code, but I haven't made this a priority to him yet, although, it looks as if his other projects will be placed on hold. This cannot continue to happen, I understand the loneliness these shifters must be feeling, but this is the wrong way to go about finding a mate for themselves.

"No, babe. I'll take care of it," I promise her.

"I'm gonna keep my eye on this site though," she emphatically informs me. Knowing her the way I do; I recognize determination in her and know there's no way I can dissuade her from doing this.

"Only observe, Glory. I mean it," I state, pointing a finger at her.

"Fine, I'll only watch. But Blaze, if I feel she's being sold off I'm gonna bid." She innocently shrugs her shoulders.

"I don't want you in the middle of this, Glory."

"Too late," she says, closing her laptop. She leans over, giving me a quick kiss and exits the room. I shake my head at her brazen balls and chuckle under my breath. I love her loyalty to her friend, but now, it seems I'll have to have Decoder keeping an eye on her and her activity.

Damn woman's gonna end up being the death of me.

TWO
BLAZE

I called Chief Anderson and told him to cancel his media briefing. When he informed me it was too late to do so, I asked that he keep us out of it, for now. Shifters will know when our name is announced as assisting, exactly who we are. We are well-known, especially in the community of supernaturals.

We're known for our ruthless ways, our take-no-shit attitudes, and every single being knows how we feel about trafficking… human and shifter alike. We will not sit idly by and let them steal humans, change them, then breed them.

Not on my damn watch. I'll fight this shit until there's no oxygen left in my lungs and my body ceases to exist.

Shifters mates are precious to them, although some grow tired of waiting to find that other missing piece of their soul. They get desperate and steal an unwilling human from the streets. That's horrible enough as it stands, but this, it's fucking ludicrous. I pick up my cell and call Kane, my VP, in for a meeting. We need to put our heads together and come up with a solid plan before bringing in our enforcers and the club's SAA.

My frame of thinking is we need to get someone inside of this organization. We need to take them down from the inside out. I send out a brief text to Kane asking him to come into my office. Getting up from my chair, I walk over to my humidifier and pull out one of my Cuban cigars. Taking my cutter, I place it on the end and cut off the tip. Luckily, being a shifter means I don't need to worry that my lungs will catch cancer from my vice.

Just as I kick back in my chair and begin to relax, a plume of smoke leaving my mouth, there's a swift knock on my door before Kane enters. He closes the door behind him then walks over to my liquor cabinet. He raises two shot glasses and my favorite bottle of whiskey in the air. I nod my head in agreement and he fills them to the rim. Walking back over to me, he hands me one then takes the seat in front of my desk. We both silently salute each other before downing our shots. The liquid fire races its way through my bloodstream. I take a puff of my cigar and prepare myself to inform my VP of what all I've been dealing with. He knows some, but he's gonna blow his top when he finds out there's things I literally haven't shared with him.

"Are you trying to keep me in suspense as to why you've summoned me to your office, Blaze?" he inquires, eyebrows raised high.

"No, but this shit is tough. It's a very touchy topic to speak on. Chief Anderson has reached out to me about women who've come up missing in our town. Just so happens, that Glory's friend from work, Angela, her daugher, Maritsa, seems to be one of the young girls who've vanished."

"Christ," Kane harshly states. "How many women are we talking about here? I know that you've reported for us to keep our eyes open for any trespassers, and that we were looking for wayward women, but why didn't you tell me all of it, Blaze?" He's understandably angry, and I feel horrible for keeping secrets, but I needed to wrap my head around this and figure out our play.

"Worldwide, or just our town? Kane, we have over a handful of girls from our town alone. Wanna know the worst part of it all?"

"There's more than just missing women we need to contend with? Isn't it bad enough that women are vanishing out of the thin blue air?" He harrumphs, crossing his arms over his chest, giving me a scathing look, one that only he can get away with. Understandable, so I let it go and don't mention it, even though my pride is taking a hit at letting this happen without reminding him exactly who's the head honcho here.

"Glory did a facial recognition something or another on Maritsa through Google. Wanna know what she discovered?" It's not really a question I'm putting out to him, it's me biding my time, trying not to lose my shit at what's been found out.

"Fucking hell, Blaze, spit it out already, would ya?" His irritation has his hands shaking as he lifts his empty glass to his mouth. Disgustingly, he roughly sets it on my desk.

"She discovered Maritsa's face on a site, a site that specifically caters to shifters. *Find your mate*, is the site's name."

"Excuse the holy hell out of me! What the fuck did you just say? Please tell me shifters are not kidnapping innocent women from the streets!"

"Wish I could, Kane. These women are being auctioned off to the highest bidder for turning and breeding purposes. Human women are being turned into animals against their will."

"That's preposterous, Blaze. This is what you've kept from me and the boys? Turning humans is against shifter law. It's only acceptable and permitted as long as the human is a mate. What the fuck are we going to do to put an end to this?"

"I'll tell ya what we're gonna do, Kane. We're going to take them down from the inside out."

"How?" he bewilderedly asks me.

"That, my friend, is what we're going to figure out. We need to get someone inside. Someone who's either already there who's willing to lend a helping hand to us, or someone that's not already affiliated with them who we believe can infiltrate them."

"We need to get Decoder on this, as quickly as possible, Blaze."

"I sent him the facial recognition that Glory did, and sent him the site she found. He's secretly working on it. I had him put all other projects on hold... for now."

Kane is an anomaly in our group. We made special accomodations for him to hold an officer patch. See, he's a jaguar, same family, different species all together. He proved himself invaluable to our club. He saved my life and the lives of several officers from other chapters once upon a time. We had a special vote and gave him a pass on not being born the 'acceptable' feline to hold a position.

It initially caused waves, but he's earned his place and showed us that he'll always go above and beyond for our club. It wasn't a popular decision, it was one we all had to fight for; but at the end of the day, our brothers would lay their lives on the line to protect him. He climbed the ranks like we all did, and earned his patch through hard work and dedication.

"Then let's get Bolt in here and fill him in. As the SAA he needs to know in order to protect the club when this shit blows the fuck up in our faces. And believe me, brother… things are about to get downright dirty."

"The fuck!" Bolt roars in anguish when he is given all the facts. "Human women being kidnapped, turned and bred! It goes against the shifter code of honor. We have to put an end to this sooner rather than later, Blaze."

"We know, Bolt, and we will. Now settle your ass down before you fry us all. Your fingers are zapping with energy," I state, as I look at his hands and notice tinges of lightning streaks dancing from the tips of his fingers.

"I'm gonna turn them all to ash," Bolt angrily states. "It's men like this that give shifters a bad reputation. It's why we hold our secrets close and don't share them with the public. They'd fear us and want to use us for scientific experiments. These are the animals that cause fear to wrack our bodies when we find mates who happen to be human. Folklore has them already skeptical of us, but these situations breed fear in humans. We'd all be burned at the damn stake like the witches of Salem if it's discovered our kind is behind these missing women."

"Keep your zapping to yourself over there, boyo," Kane pointedly looks at Bolt. He looks ready to jump and haul ass at a moment's notice if Bolt's fingers begin to produce more energetic, lengthy streaks than the tiny zaps of electricity that are dancing from finger to finger. Bolt shakes his hands in the air, then closes his eyes and concentrates on pulling the currents back into his body. When he has control of himself, he opens his eyes and nods his head at me.

"I'm good," he promises. "Now, we need to find out who all is inside and who we can buy out. There's no way this late in the game we can find someone to fit in and become entrusted with inside knowledge of the operation. In my personal opinion, that's our best hope."

"Kane, go get with Decoder and see where he's at. Let him know what we want him looking for. There has to be someone desperate enough for money to betray the organizers. I want to know how high up this goes; we need to chop the head off the head snake so the rest will crumble."

"We are taking them all out, though, correct?" Bolt asks the question.

"Abso-fucking-lutely," I tell him. "I need to shift, either one of you wanna join me?"

"Damn straight," Bolt declares.

"Right behind ya," Kane adds. "I'm gonna stop by and give Decoder your orders before joining y'all. Won't be long."

We take off our clothes once we hit the back acreage. True to Kane's words, he wasn't but a minute or two behind us. We have miles and miles of terrain at our fingertips. We don't worry about trespassers, the town fears us and knows better than to step foot on our property.

As soon as my body begins reforming and my bones break to make way for my leopard, I close my eyes and allow the magic of my transformation take hold. I love the way my shift happens… I don't feel the pain much anymore, it's something I've become accustomed to.

The power that takes hold of my mind with my feline fellow counterpart, is indescribable. The sense of empowerment and indestructability, always gives me a feeling of coming home.

After the last few days I've had, it feels good to stretch my paws and dig my nails into earth's dirt. The three of us race, jumping over fallen trees, chasing wildlife and catching a snack. I climb up a tree and rest myself on a limb as I watch Kane and Bolt's cats enjoy the freedom that comes with their shift. They are both big cats, not as big as mine seeing as I'm Alpha born, but intimidating enough to anyone who crosses their path.

I begin grooming myself, cleaning off the dirt and debris from my padded paws. As I sit here thinking, my mind travels to my mate and what she may be getting herself into. I need to bring her out for a run, just the two of us. It's been awhile since we've frolicked and played. I miss her cat, my cat misses hers, he lets out a yowl of longing.

Soon, I promise him.

This pacifies him temporarily, but it's a promise I have to keep or he could shed my skin, without permission from me, and seek out his mate. We have to let our leopards out to play with one anothers or they grow restless and can potentially become uncontrollable.

GLORY

I've been keeping an eye on the website. I've come in as an anonymous bidder on Maritsa. I've rerouted my IP address to where it looks as if I'm making inquiries on her from overseas. My hope is that if I can win her bid, then I can give the location for the pick-up to the guys.

They are looking at the bigger picture; my goal is to free my friend's daughter and let the rest of the pieces fall apart once the men get involved.

I've been splitting my time between work at the school, taking care of Angela, doing my duties as the old lady of the president, plus making sure the homestead stays maintained. I'm doing three people's jobs, and at the end of the day, I'm a walking, talking zombie.

Blaze has been taking his anguish out on my body every night, but I feel as if I've let him down by basically being a third party to our lovemaking. I'm there physically, but my mind is always elsewhere. If he's noticed, he hasn't said anything to me. But that's the spectacular thing about mates.

We know when to push a topic, and when to just show our love and support to one another and let the other one work out what's plaguing their mind. Relationships are all about give and take, and these days, we're both taking what we need from the other and giving the other the space needed to work through our turmoils.

Today, I'm solely concentrating on the bidding. Maritsa is up, and I can't take my eyes off the competitors for even a split second. I may get outbid and that cannot happen. Her life as she knows it is at stake if I do.

I hope she makes it out of this situation alive, human, and willing to never speak of the things she's witnessed and heard while in captivity. If she's a threat to our kind, we'll have no choice but to turn her so that she will keep our closely guarded secret. If her life is on the line along with the rest of ours, she'll have to be proactive to stay living.

All of these human women who've been kidnapped will have to be vetted before we can allow them to go back home to their human families. It's going to be a long process and we'll have to find a shifter therapist to help them overcome the tragedy they've been trapped in.

When Maritsa's bid hits half a million dollars, I pick up my phone and text Blaze. He needs to be here to give me permission to outbid this person. The club will have to fund it, he and I don't have that kind of money at our disposal. He texts me back immediately letting me know that I do not need to place another bid, that the other person is Decoder bidding on the club's behalf. I chuckle at the fact that I was willing to go up against the club unwittingly. Leave it to my man and the club to be full of shocking surprises.

I knew Blaze wouldn't let this go, but I had no clue he'd go to the extent of bidding for Maritsa's survival. I've checked in on Angela as much as she'll allow me to, but she's recently been declining, becoming a shell of the woman she once was. Even a short time ago, she was in a fighting stance, now, she stares out into oblivion when I'm around. She only has a one-track mind these days;

locating and finding her daughter. I feel like a horrible friend for not telling her what I know, but I can't. It's as if she knows I'm keeping something from her and is punishing me by not speaking to me unless spoken to.

My heart breaks, but there's nothing I can do to comfort her, other than be there to hold her hand through this debacle. It would put a price on my head within the shifter community if I was to divulge that information to her. I wouldn't be the only one either; Angela, along with Blaze, would also be looking over their shoulders. I can't, and won't, do that to my old man.

He's my life; the day we crossed paths at a shifter retreat is the best day of my life. We knew immediately that the other was our mate; our senses were on high alert. We were magnetically drawn to each other instantly, the need to consummate was overwhelming.

Humans wouldn't understand the sense of urgency we had to mark each other. Claim the other one with the other one's scent. My memory floats into an oblivious state as the day resurfaces to flood the forefront of my mind.

THREE
GLORY

TEN YEARS EARLIER

"Jax, slow down!" I yell at my childhood friend. He's excited to connect with female shifters today, hoping that this will be the year that he finds his true mate.

"Come on, Glory! Aren't you excited to meet the single men from other groups? This is the year, I feel it," he exclaims excitedly. "I just know the two of us are gonna walk away this year with our mate by our sides."

"Well, aren't you the optimistic one," I chuckle as my nose wrinkles with a scent that's enchanting to my senses. Sandalwood, musk and chocolate! My three favorite things in the world. "Do you smell that, Jax?" He stops, lifts his face into the air, catching the breeze around us. He shakes his head negatively and looks at me as if I've grown a second head.

"What are you smelling, Glory? I smell the sunshine and fresh breeze in the air. Wait," he sniffs again, "is that cotton candy?"

"Jax, there's no cotton candy vendors here... I think your sense of smell is off," I joke around with him. Other than the smells I indicated earlier; barbeque being grilled permeates the air around us. "No, it's there," he once again insists.

"Then you should follow your nose," I direct him. "I'm gonna do the same." I leave him to follow his own trail as I continue on the path that mine is leading me down. This would be so much easier in leopard form; but there is an unwritten rule about shifting in public; even at one of our own held events. The scent gets stronger the closer I get to the beer tent. I feel my skin prickle and my fangs elongate from my gums. Mine, my leopard whispers in my mind. That could only mean one thing, my mate is here!

Just then, I feel a warm breath scenting my neck from behind me. Then words are whispered that send a shockwave of emotions through my system, "Where've you been all of my life?"

"Waiting for you to find me." I twirl around and stare into my mate's eyes. They're as green as emeralds sparkling in the rays of the sun. His hair is as blond as the driven snow. He's built like a bodybuilder and has tattoos covering every square inch of his arms that's visible outside of his tight, form framing T-shirt.

"Well, I've found you now. You'll never get away from me now that I have." His eyes blaze with lust as he states this to me. "What's your name, mate?"

"Glory," I all but whimper out, as my overzealous hormones surge out of control through my bloodstream. "You?"

"Blaze," he huskily states, oblivious to how he's profoundly affecting me. His voice causes my legs to quiver as I fight to keep them steady and hold my body in an upright position.

"How appropriate," I stammer out, causing him to throw his head back in laughter. My eyes stay glued to his Adam's apple as it bobs in his throat. My mouth salivates with the deepest desire to lick and strike that particular spot with my mating claim. My teeth are ready, my body is strung tightly, my saliva is forming in readiness to sink my essence into him. He'll reek of me and no other female shifter will ever go near him. That's the best thing about our kind, we don't poach on other's mates. It's as if they're put off by the scent of another's pheromones combined with each other.

"Don't worry, my Glory. We won't be going down in any blazes of fire," he assures me, as we each move a little closer to the other. I begin to chuckle at his words, yeah, I had that thought dancing around in my mind. How astute that we'd have the same sense of humor.

"You've got that title wrong, big guy," I inform him as he lifts his hand to cup my cheek. "It's Blaze of Glory."

"Well, either way, the only thing that'll be catching fire tonight, and the rest of our lives, is the linens that make up our mated bed." I want to roll my eyes at his cliche'd words, but they're too damn cute so I keep from outwardly displaying this.

"When?" I ask, swiping my tongue along my bottom lip.

"Not until our mating ceremony, Glory. We must respect our prides, and their beliefs. I will always hold you in the highest regards and only show you the respect you deserve as my mate, and old lady."

"Old lady?" I inquire, confused. "And you did just now say tonight, or did I hear that wrong?" I'm only nineteen, nowhere near needing hair dye to cover the gray at the root of my head nor a cane for balance as I walk.

"I'm in line for presidency of the Dark Leopards MC. I've been in the club one way or another my entire life," Blaze admits. I can see the trepidation in his face, the worry is deep that I won't accept this part of him. My gut burns at the thought that anyone would be willing to give up their true mate because of something as trivial as what the other does for a living. Because at the end of the day, that's his job.

"*Mate,*" Blaze calls out at me through our mating link. "*Is there a reason we're reliving this day in particular?*"

"*I was just thinking about the day we met.*" I leave out the 'best day of my life' part. My man already has a swollen head when it comes to us and his prowess when it comes to his manhood and our relationship. Looking back at the screen, seeing Maritsa's picture, I begin to feel a longing for the day that Blaze and I will have children, cubs of our very own.

Something is always coming up with the club, causing him to want to push it off a little longer. But I'm always yearning to become a mother, my maternal clock is ticking. I find myself becoming more restless as each day passes with the need to mother a cub of my own.

"*Mate, you just went quiet, is everything okay?*" His worried tone brings me out of my musings.

"*Yeah, Blaze. Everything's alright,*" I lie through my teeth as I say this to him. It's why I usually resort to texting him instead of using our link; he has this innate ability to know when something's bothering me.

"*Please don't shut me out, Glory. I can feel that something's weighing heavily on your mind.*"

"*I promise, Blaze. I'm really okay. Just worried about Maritsa and the way it's affecting Angela.*"

"We'll get her back, I swear it, Glory."

"And the other women? Blaze, their families must be terribly worried."

"We're gonna do what we can. I swear this to you, Glory. I won't rest until they're all home; safe and sound." Him taking on the world is what worries me the most. He's always playing savior to everyone else and leaving me barren.

"I believe you, Blaze."

BLAZE

She may think she's hiding her sorrows from me; but I know that she's been wallowing in her grief of me not giving her any cubs. I watch her as she watches the kids play in the clubhouse, how her eyes fall each time they leave to head home with their parents. I ache to give her the deepest desires of the heart; but when we have cubs, I want to make sure they come into our lives at a time when the club is at peace.

We won't always have harmony; but I want to parent my children, not be that co-parent that is sometimes around and available. I want to be an integral part of their upbringing, bandage scraped knees, teach them to play ball and ride their bicycles… then later, upgrade to their very own hog.

Maybe it's time to reconsider my point of view on this topic; as the president, I'm always going to be in demand where it pertains to the club. I can figure out a way to merge the two into one and be the parent I've always wanted to be. My woman, my mate, has been patient with me as I come to terms with businesses and endeavors the club is involved with or what we support for the other chapters.

My own memories of the day we met surface and I find that a smile graces my face. Best damn day of my life the day my nose smelled her and my beast found her in the crowd.

We walk through the fair grounds that the shifters have rented for this festival of sorts. It's our annual 'find your mate' fair that young shifters attend in the hopes of finding the one that was born to complete you. The other half of your soul that the other person was born holding in their possession.

"Did you always want to be the president of the Dark Leopards MC?" she asks, as we walk side by side, hands intertwined with each others.

"I wouldn't say want, as much as I would state born for the role and position. My father is the president now, but he's ready to step aside and let me take over. He's just waiting for my twenty-fifth birthday to come."

"So, you have to what? Be that age to take that position?" Her mind is rapidly scanning for questions, don't ask me how I know this, I just seem to feel it in the marrow of my bones.

"No. But that's when Pops is comfortable handing the club over to me to run. I'm good with that, I don't feel ready to be in control of finances, businesses, or brothers and the trouble they all seem to find themselves in at one time or another."

"Are they rowdy? Your brothers?" That's a loaded question if I've ever heard one. How do I answer that without scaring her away before I get the opportunity to lay my claim properly on her?

"They're men, sweetheart. Young, dumb and full of cum," I express, waggling my eyebrows at her as I say this. "Just typical bullshit really. Nothing too serious, but immaturity is branded into them with their lack of life experiences behind them."

"Makes sense. Jax is a little on the nutty side as well," she nonchalantly states, but all I want to know is who this Jax fucker is and if I'm gonna have to bury him six-feet under. She must feel my body tense because she goes on to say, "Don't worry, Jax is no threat to you, Blaze. We grew up together, our fathers are best friends who also grew up together. It's a family thing to where the cubs become besties," she teases me, causing all the tension to leave my body. Her voice carries a melodic tune through the air to my ears from her sweet, sensual voice. "Well, they were best *friends before my father decided he wanted to be a one-man den."*

I choose not to broach the subject further on her father, it seems to be one that upsets and hurts her. I don't want our first day together to be filled with painful memories.

"So, the past two generations have birthed best friends I'm taking it." She laughs, nodding her head yes. "My best friend is in the Marines. He left right out of high school and I haven't seen him since. We wrote letters back and forth for a few years, but life sorta got in the way. He married another soldier and had twin cubs within a year. I still hear from him every now and then, but not as often as I'd like to."

"He found his mate in the Corps? That's amazing, Blaze. We never know when we'll meet that person or under what circumstances. I bet it's hard to serve our country and still keep a marriage and family intact."

"Yeah. He's a leopard like me and she's a unique albino panther. Their cubs are beautiful little girls. He sent me a photo last Christmas of the family in front of a tree. To be honest with you, I was kind of jealous that he'd already found his mate and started his family while I was prospecting; cleaning shit from toilets and patched members' vomit up after parties." Her eyes widen upon my confession then she sticks her tongue out and makes an 'ack' sound. "It's not the prettiest of jobs, but we all have to serve our time to gain our patch and position within the ranks."

"Are those days over for you, Blaze?" She stops walking and looks up at me with the bluest eyes I've ever seen. *Her auburn hair is whipping in the air from the breeze and her lithe, athletic body hones true to the animal she's harboring inside of her. I want to lick every inch of her, map out her body and seal the memories in a vault inside my mind.*

"As of two weeks ago, they are. I received my patch and member's cut. Best day of my life other than today," I admit, watching as her eyes glaze over once my words penetrate. *I know we're both struggling to keep our hands and teeth to ourselves, it's hard for mates upon meeting. Our instincts are to claim and announce to the world that the other is off limits. Not to mention, our hormones and animals are raging, clawing with need inside of us, to seal the bond.*

"It's good to know I rank up there pretty high," she jests, as we both break out into peals of laughter.

My memories are interrupted by the ringing of my cell phone. Reaching into my desk drawer, I pull it up and look at the display. The caller ID shows that it's Chief Anderson calling. "Fuck, this can't be good."

Closing my eyes for a brief second, I hit the green phone button, answering the call. "Chief, what can I do for you today?"

"We have a problem, Blaze. You may want to make sure you're sitting when I share this new development with you."

And just like that, my recently acquired good mood vanishes.

FOUR
BLAZE

After hanging up with the Chief, I called both Bolt and Kane asking them to come into my office. By the time they arrive, I'm well on my way into a fit of uncontrollable rage.

"What's going on, Blaze?" Kane asks as he heads over to my liquor cabinet, pouring himself a shot of brandy. My stock is low, so he's having to settle for that brand of liquor; not his favorite, but he can tell by the expression on my face he's gonna need something stronger than beer for this conversation.

"Am I gonna need one of those too?" Bolt asks as he eyes the shot glass in Kane's hand.

"We're all gonna need one, or the bottle," I mumble out my frustration with this situation. "One of our victims was found deceased. Her throat had basically been ripped out."

"In other words, someone tried to change her and she struggled with the bite," Bolt insinuates as his fingers begin to twitch. Kane and I warily watch him as he gains control of himself. Kane always wears gloves because he too has issues with his hands and touch… only his will shock you, not shoot lightning bolts through you.

"That's the only conclusion I could come up with too." I concur with Bolt's assessment. It's the only thing that makes any damn sense. There's no other reason for that type of injury to occur outside of that. Not unless this predator's intent was to chase and capture, not bed and breed.

"Has Decoder been able to come up with anything on his end?" Kane asks me. I see him struggle to contain his composure; he feels things deeply. Deeper than the rest of us, and I can't help but worry about him the most out of all my men.

"So far, all of the towers the website has pinged from have been different locations. He's tried to follow each and every one of them, but it's gonna take a while," I answer Kane's question to the best of my capabilities. I don't understand anything technical… Decoder talks to me and it goes in one ear and out the other.

"If these women are fighting back, I expect we'll be seeing more dead bodies showing up," Bolt announces, taking his shot and downing it.

"I agree, we need to get an in," I state. Just as those words leave my mouth, Decoder comes barrelling into the room.

"Got 'em, Pres," he states, placing his laptop in front of me. Bolt and Kane come over and stand directly behind me as we watch Decoder scan through his computer, going from one page to another page. "I was able to find the codes to break into their mainframe."

"Speak English, boyo, ain't none of us intellectual when it comes to technical jargon," Kane explicits through a tone bordering on disgust. "I've already got a headache coming on, and you've just begun spewing out shit."

"Sorry, Pres, VP." Decoder slows down and takes a deep breath before continuing. "I was able to jump through their firewalls on their servers, which is set up to protect them from discovery." Kane nods his head for him to continue. "The mainframe is the computer's mind; it recalls and holds in memory everything that's been submitted throughout the history of that computer and site. After following the IP addresses as they switched from one tower and server to another; I was finally able to trace it to one person or persons as it turns out."

"Decoder, spit that shit out already. I don't like playing detective and having to read between the lines and shit. Just give me a damn name already," I venomously hiss out, ready to put this all behind us. I want to stop the disappearance of innocent women who are bordering on adulthood.

They haven't had an opportunity to live their lives as young as they are. They've had their choices stolen from them and are being introduced into a life that they weren't aware even existed. It's got to be terrifying for them; these are the situations nightmares are made of. And I plan on being the one who pulls them from the depths of hell.

"You remember that band of rogue shifters we came upon three or so years ago?" he inquires, with a lifted eyebrow.

"The bear, lion, wolf and snake? That was an odd breed of friends if I've ever seen any. Why? Fuck me, you have got to be yanking my chain! Those cretins are behind this?" I'm fit to be tied; those fuckers were run out of our town because they were on a 'mate' finding mission. They were groping our women, and terrorizing our town. The club banded together and escorted them to the border.

"The one and the same," Decoder insist. "They are behind this; from the conversations they've had online,

I've been able to determine that they scoured the country, looking for shifters who've been unlucky in finding their mate."

"But those imbeciles aren't smart enough to put an operation of this magnitude together," Bolt declares through a snort of disbelief.

"They have to have a financial backer." I state my thoughts out loud. "Those fuckers didn't have the money to finance something as big as this. It takes some serious dough to be able to house, feed and run a program catering to women."

"Who would be wealthy enough as well as stupid enough to back these morons?" Kane questions, almost to himself. I can tell he's deep in thought. We all quietly go through possibilities in our head until Decoder clears his throat.

"Well, that's the thing," Decoder states, flipping to another tab pinned to the top of his screen. "They have three backers; pretty high up fuckers who are loaded."

"Jesus fucking Christ," I spit out, worrying over how we can take on not one, but three wealthy, well-connected pieces of shit.

"Our own state representative, Jason Glemson. Attorney General Markus Carmichael and a member of our elite shifter councilmen." Bolt, Kane and I jump when he states the last one... someone who's responsible for the safety and welfare of our people has betrayed every shifter in the world.

"Who?" I grit out, ready to fucking destroy members of our own society.

"Anston Greyhorse," he hesitantly states. The reason behind his hesitation is because Anston was my father's best friend and is a club confidant. He's kept us out of trouble numerous times with the council when we've gone above and beyond what they deem acceptable behavior. We've had to do some shady things that go against the shifter code and law to ensure the safety of our own.

"I need to call my pops. He'll know how to handle the council without any blowback on us. Keep digging, Decoder; get me as much information as you can. We'll meet back up once I have a chance to get Pops here. I'd like you all to be here for that meeting." They all stand up and exit the room. Wondering how I'm going to ultimately approach this topic with Pops, I simply send him a text asking when he can make it to the clubhouse for an impromptu meeting.

GLORY

Feeling a bit guilty for causing Blaze to worry over my grief, I decide to make him a gourmet meal for dinner.

One fit for a king, or a president; depending on how you look at it. My mate is a sucker for a good home cooked Italian meal. Bringing out my press, I begin making, from scratch, noodles for lasagna. Once that task is done, I begin shredding cheese and humming one of my favorite songs as I shake my hips to the beat in my head. I feel arms wrap around me from behind. I jump, placing my hand over my chest as I attempt to get my breathing under control. "Blaze, you scared the absolute shit out of me," I huff while berating myself for being careless enough not to notice his entry.

"Sorry, babe. What did I do so fantastic to get a meal of this magnitude? I'm asking, because I wanna make sure I do it again," he jests with me. Even though he's teasing, I feel like a bad mate for not taking care of his needs through this ordeal. He has a lot riding on his shoulders as it is, now all of this kidnapping stuff is taking precedence over his normal MC duties.

"I realized today that I haven't been taking proper care of you. Look at you," I say smacking his abs, "you're practically wasting away." He places his hand over mine, where it's still resting against his stomach, then leans down and pecks me on top of my head.

"I believe that's gone both ways, Glory," he huskily responds, as his lips travel down my head and the cord of my neck. He goes back up and ends up breathing into my ear, I get shivers running up and down my arms, then he nips my ear lobe with his teeth. "Tonight, it's just us, baby. After you take care of me, I plan on taking care of you." His words cause anticipation to slither throughout my body. My knees grow weak as my heartbeat ramps up, practically beating its way out of my chest cavity and making a roaring sound in my ears.

"I absolutely love that idea, it's a splendid plan actually," I purr; my cat loves the idea too. She's clawing inside of me, wanting to skip our dinner and go right to the dessert portion of the evening.

"Spectacular, after we feed the rumbling beast," he states, patting his stomach. "I'll fulfill my taste buds with your sweet nectar for dessert."

"Why don't you go relax in the living room and I'll bring you out a beer?" I suggest, needing a moment to gather my composure. "Or would you rather have a glass of whiskey?"

"It's a relaxing and beer type of night," he explains. "I'll fill you in later. Right now, I just want to unwind and spend some quality time with my mate."

"Dinner will be ready in an hour; I believe there's a ball game or two on tonight. Why don't you go chill out with one? It's been a while since you've been able to enjoy a good game on the television," I suggest, knowing that if not, he'll sit in there and ponder everything that's happened over the last few weeks.

Two hours later, dinner has been consumed. Blaze and I are sitting in front of the television as the ballgame concludes. His team lost, but it hasn't seemed to sour his mood any. "Why don't you go start a bath, fill it with your scentsy, girly shit you like, and I'll join you in a few?"

"Why, mate, are you offering to soak in the tub with me?" I bat my eyelashes at him, making my efforts to entertain him successful when he chuckles. "It's been a while since we've soaked together and just talked."

"And that's where we need to begin, tonight. Enjoying each other's company and reconnecting with one another." The sincerity in his tone has me swooning like a teenage girl whose crush just spoke to her for the first time.

"Love you, my bearly mate." Reaching over, I plant a hasty kiss to his lips and scurry out of the room.

"Love you too! And I'm not a damn bear, woman. I'm a motherfucking predator, a fierce cat! People run for shelter and safety when they see me coming!" I chuckle as he hollers these words out to me.

FIVE
GLORY

Once the water is at the perfect temperature, I put the stopper down into the drain, and add a layer of my relaxing lavender scented bubbles into it. The fragrance immediately hits my senses and I quickly undress myself. I've always been *that* woman who enjoys sitting in the water as it fills in around her. Reaching over to the lip of the tub, I grab my hair tie and throw it up into a sloppy bun on top of my head. If my man and I are going to have sexy time afterward, I don't want to have wet hair. He loves my hair hanging loose as we tumble around in the bed.

Not once since we've been together, have we made love, fucked, had sex, without him running his beefy hands through my long, layered locks. I once threatened to cut it off to my shoulders and you would've thought that war had been declared. He vehemently put his foot down and demanded that I no longer entertain the thought. Instead, I just pile it up on top of my head when I don't wanna mess with it.

He can tell even when I trim the dead ends off... he pays that close of attention to me and my body. I shiver when memories surface of the way he controls me with his hands buried in my hair. He has this way of dominating me and I love everything he's done. He's inventive and finds new ways each time we're intimate to bring me to my knees.

That Alpha part of him is more predominate in the bedroom than outside of it. I see the way his men fall in line when he issues an order, and I do the exact same thing in the bedroom.

Closing my eyes; I sink into the water and allow it to run over my feet. When I was a little cub, I used to pretend I was in a waterfall. I've always read about them in books, but have never seen one in real life. So I always allowed my imagination to take me there. Soft rock begins to play quietly in the background; and a smile begins to form on my face. He's in true fashion tonight, playing the romantic card. I enjoy these types of nights; cuddled in his arms and the two of us letting the world's worries melt away as I lose myself in him... in us.

We've always managed to connect on a level that's blown my mind. I knew mates were supposed to instantaneously connect, but I never imagined the intensity of it until Blaze entered my life.

"Got room for one more in there, love?" I feel his heated breath on the base of my neck as he whispers these words into my ear.

"I've always got room for you. And if not, we'll always make some," I say, opening my eyes and getting mesmerized by the way his are laced with the heat and intensity of an inferno. They're full of lust and cause my middle to ache in need. I've been in his bed, had him between my thighs nearly every night, but tonight feels so different… much more intense.

"You have a wicked tongue and words spun of pure gold, mate," he huskily states as he lifts me forward; sliding down behind me. His arms wrap around me, pulling me snugly against the front of his chest. "Just how naughty and sinful can that tongue of yours get, Glory?" My tongue, so much I can do with it to his appendage and muscles. I dream of what all I can do to cause him to ultimately lose control of his limbs and being.

An uncontrolled Blaze is a sight I always long to witness.

"There are no words yet discovered, nor placed in the English dictionary, to describe how nefarious my tongue can get, Blaze," I find myself once again purring words out to him. "But, my words speak volumes through actions."

"Oh, my mate," he says, nuzzling his face into my neck, "how I know that to be the accurate truth."

"Will a demonstration be in order tonight, Blaze?" There are no descriptive words to be used at the tone I'm portraying with these words.

"Without a doubt," he responds, nipping the skin between my shoulder blade and my neck. His hardness is protruding against my back, and I find myself scissoring my legs back and forth with a desperate need for relief. His hand glides down the front of my stomach, landing at the juncture between my thighs. "Let's see how needy we can make you before making it to our bed."

"I'm already desperate for you, mate," I admit as my hand comes over his, cupping it. I begin to grind into our joined hands, putting pressure on top of his. "My core is aching with need for you to fill me."

"Like this?" He inserts a finger, but holds it still and unmoving inside of me.

"Mmm… close, Blaze. You've almost got it."

"Then you want this," he declares, placing a second finger inside of me, slowly and methodically pumping them in and out of my weeping pussy. "Your body is desperately trying to hold my fingers hostage, mate. Feel how tightly you're clamping down on my digits. I can't wait to insert my cock in there." His words, followed by his actions, nearly spiral me into an orgasm. He slowly removes his fingers, and lightly grazes the lips of my labia. He finds my protruding nub, barely skimming it before going back down and circling my entrance. "You have such a greedy cunt."

"Only for you, Blaze. Always, only for you," I stammer out, as desperation takes hold. "Please, Blaze, stop teasing me."

"Anticipation will only make you that much more hungry for my cock later." Whereas this is a true statement, and normally I'd go along with it; it's been a bit since we've been intimate with one another and I need him inside of me, like a desperate hussy. We've had sex, but that's all it was, I want to see his eyes as they burn into mine. I want to feel with the touch of his fingers how desperately he needs me. I want to feel his chest slicken with sweat as he pounds relentlessly inside of me.

"Blaze…" I'm ready to beg and plead, as if my life and very being depends on it. At this point, I'm ready to explode and take matters into my own hands.

"Patience, mate. It's time for me to take care of you. Lean forward so I can start by washing your back." Deciding that having his hands on me in any way is worth it, instead of arguing with him, I lean forward. He takes my loofah and suds it up with my feminine body wash.

His hands lazily glide along my skin, not missing an inch of my body as he makes sure every square inch of my skin is clean. He saves my tits and pussy for last. I stand in the tub, putting the apex of my thighs directly in front of his nose. He heavily breathes in my intoxicating, calling of the mate, scent as he reaches up, washing my breasts. He plays with my nipples, causing them to stand into tall peaks. As his hand makes its way down my stomach, the muscles tighten from his touch. He leans forward and pushes my thighs open wider with his hands.

"Fuck, but my need to taste you, then mount you, is overwhelming."

"Yes." Are the only words I'm capable of forming at his husky, needy filled proclamation.

BLAZE

Fuck, how my mate is a temptress. I wanted to take things slow and be sensual and loving with her, but she makes things hard for me to contain myself and maintain my composure.

I want tonight to be special for her. Tonight, we will begin our journey of bringing a cub into our family. There will be no latex between us, only our skin as it burns for the simple touch of the other. This will be the night that I start to give her that part of me that her heart's been desiring.

Our lives will never be one hundred percent safe enough to add an addition, I'll just have to ensure their safety with the help of the club and my brothers. I thought long and hard about this as I sat in front of the television tonight. She's always worked hard to give me the best life a man could hope for, it's time for me to return that favor to her.

My job, as her mate and old man, is to fulfill all of her dreams and watch her soar as they come to fruition. Watching her eyes dim as she watches all of the other children leave takes my breath away... how can I deprive her of motherhood? I can't, I won't.

Not anymore, not ever again.

This picture-perfect life I've envisioned bringing a cub into isn't reality based. As soon as that recognition hit me in the face, I began thinking about it in other ways. I'm a protector by nature, so I can surely find a way to make this happen. I may not be there for every bump and bruise, but I'll be there for all of the important things in life.

As soon as she's clean, I help her out of the tub and head for the shower. "Meet me in the room, baby."

"I'll be there, ready and waiting." She winks at me as I enter the steamy stream of water. I quickly wash and get out. Toweling myself dry, I walk into the room as I'm scrubbing one over my head. Looking up, I see Glory spread out like an angel on our bed.

"Damn," I utter, taking in the beauty that is perfectly displayed out before me. "You are the very picture of perfection."

"You have to say that," she shyly insist.

"When have I ever said something I don't wholeheartedly agree with? You know me better than that, beautiful."

"Instead of talking, why don't you come show me." She bites her bottom lip, enticing me to throw caution to the wind and say 'fuck it' to taking things slow. Her need is matching my own, we can take our time with each other… later.

Much later.

I crawl up the bed and rest my fingers over her nipples. I love their raspberry color and the large discs where her nipples protrude from. I use one hand to nip and pull on one while my mouth rests firmly over the other. My tongue licks around it then I suck it deeply into my mouth. Her legs come up and wrap around my hips as her back arches off the bed. She's always been sensitive to nipple play; it arouses her to the point where she can barely contain herself.

Just a tad bit out of control and wild is how I love my mate to be. I lift my upper body across hers and plant my lips over hers. Our tongues meet as my hips gyrate, keeping up with the timing of my mouth. The actions are nearly in perfect sync with one another. My dick slides through her slick slit, coating me in her liquid essence.

With a desperate need to connect with my mate, I slide my hand between us until it grabs purchase of the root of my stone hard dick. I line myself up with her opening and slide deeply inside of her. My balls thrash against her ass as my dick pummels in and out of her passage. Removing my lips from hers, I place my face at the nape of her neck. "Fucking heaven," I whisper, eliciting chill bumps where I've spoken.

"We're flawless together, this is perfection," she cries out as I slam myself inside. "I love you so much, Blaze."

"I love you too, my beautiful mate." Needing to mount her, just like I did on the night we claimed one another and every night in between, I remove myself from her depths and help her roll over to her front. "Hands and knees, beautiful Glory, I need to see that delectable ass of yours as my dick devours your pussy."

"Yes, fuck yes," she growls as she lifts her lower end high up in the air. My hands lift up and squeeze each globe, loving the contrast between my hands and the cheeks of her ass. It's so tempting to reach down and take a chunk out of her, but my dick is calling the shots here and wants to feel the warmth of her internal heat as it wraps around him.

As I penetrate her, a sense of belonging and welcoming invades my person; it's our bond, reminding us that we are meant and made for each other. As I slide back inside of her, I begin a relentless, pounding pace. I look down and see her claiming bite mark. Not being able to resist, I lean over and open my jaw wide, my teeth grow as I break through her skin. A moan of ecstasy is released from her mouth as she clamps down on my shaft.

It's so hard that it almost feels like her body is fearful of releasing me. She wants to own me just as much as I own her, if not more. I release my teeth from her shoulder and seal the wound shut with my tongue.

"My turn," she announces as she lifts her body up, dislodging me from her.

Knowing what she wants, I lay down on my back and grab a hold of her hips as she lines herself up with me. She slowly lowers herself down, pleasure spikes through my body as I finally hit balls deep. She begins to ride me to the point that my eyes roll into the back of my sockets. Before I realize what is happening, she clamps her teeth into my neck. Ropes of come shoot out of me from the enjoyment of her re-claiming.

We find our release together, shouting one another's names as darkness consumes us both. We pass out with me still deeply embedded inside of her core.

Later that night, our human halves and our cat halves, are lazily lying in the sated afterglow of love making. No matter how quick and hasty I take her, or if I'm slow and sensual, it's always making love in my heart. Glory is sound asleep in my arms; after the first round of taking her without a condom, we ended up talking about our future and I informed her that I was ready to become a father. Tears pricked in her eyes before her lips landed in a crushing kiss on mine. Our second round was full of passion as we lit the sheets on fire. Our hands roamed each other's flesh, our eyes stayed glued to each other's as we shared words of endearment.

Hearing my phone ding with an incoming text, I climb out of the warmth of my woman and head toward my pants laying on the floor. Pulling it out of my pocket, I notice it's a response from my pops.

Was out on the lake fishing. Just got your message, will be at the clubhouse first thing in the morning. Sending him a thumbs up emoji, I take my phone with me and plug it into the charger on my nightstand. I'll send my officers a message in the morning letting them know they need to be in my office. They're never far from the clubhouse no matter the time of the day and I'm not wanting to message them now in case they're sleeping. Getting a phone call this late in the evening will have them restless the rest of the night and I need them refreshed and alert. There's no telling how my pops is going to take the news of his friend's ultimate betrayal.

SIX
BLAZE

The next morning comes all too quickly. I left my woman sleeping and sated in my warm bed while I come to the clubhouse. I need to mentally get myself prepared for the uncomfortable conversation I'll be forced to have with Pops.

Anston Greyhorse, you motherfucker. I hope they burn you at the stake for your part in this.

I always trusted him with the club's utmost confidence; the low blow from his actions have me seething red with anger. I have tunnel vision and can't wait for the day to come that he has to pay penance for his involvement with those slimy weasels.

Having already called Kane and Bolt in for the meeting, I head into the kitchen to make myself a cup of coffee. I would love to be able to insert some whiskey in it, but

I'll need my head clear later. Once I have a cup in hand, I walk back to my office and stop in the door jamb when I see Pops sitting at my desk.

"Hey, Son." He stands up, walks around my desk and over to me. He embraces me in a fatherly hug, making me wish he was here solely for a father and son catch up visit with me.

"Hey, Pops. We're just waiting on Kane and Bolt to join us. Wanna cup?" I ask, lifting my mug in his direction.

"Nah," he says patting his belly. "Your mom made me a hearty breakfast this morning and I've already had a pot of that," he chuckles.

"I sometimes forget what an early bird Ma is. I left Glory sound asleep in our bed this morning. I'd have loved to have had breakfast with her before starting the day off."

"One day, Son, when you both retire, you'll be able to do that and more," he wiggles his eyebrows at me causing me to spew my coffee that I'd just taken a sip of.

"No. Just no. I don't want to think about you and Ma like that." I do an exaggerated body shiver, causing him to throw his head back and laugh.

"What did we miss?" Kane asks as he and Bolt join us, shutting the door behind them as they walk in.

"Pops was just sharing about his alone time with Ma." My eyes widen as I turn my head in his direction. All but begging him with that look to change the topic of conversation.

"I don't know if I should be throwing up at that, or high fiving you, Pops," Bolt states.

"I personally feel as if I vomited in my mouth a little," Kane retorts, and his look is anything but joking.

"I feel ya there, brother." Suddenly, I feel the need to go surf the web and see if they have a memory eraser available in pill form. This is one conversation I never expected to have with Pops.

"You're a bunch of pussies," Pops declares. "Never thought I'd live to see the day that my boys became all girly." He wiggles his fingers at us in a ladylike fashion.

"Can we change the subject?" Bolt inquires. "I'd personally like to diminish the thoughts running through my head."

"Amen. There's something about one's parents a kid should never be privy to," I state, giving Pops a narrow-eyed glare.

"Fine, fine. The bunch of you are pansy asses. What did you bring me here for?" Pops asks, walking back around the desk and taking my seat… again. I want to remind him he's retired and that's my position of authority, but

I have a feeling he'll need that comfort and security to deal with the things he's fixing to learn.

"Pops, this is hard for me to say." I swallow the saliva that's formed in my throat. "Anston, he's not who we believed him to be." Pops leans forward in his chair, his eyebrows are extended to his hairline as he awaits for me to further explain my declaration of his friend. Gathering my composure, I continue, "The club's been dealing with missing women... human women, the oldest so far is twenty years old. Decoder has been working hard to obtain any leads by following the breadcrumbs on the dark web. Do you remember the bear, lion, wolf and snake shifters we had problems with in town not too long ago?" He nods his head in acknowledgement but doesn't otherwise utter a single word. "They're the front men of the operation, they are the ones who go out scouring the towns and ultimately kidnapping the women." Pops grounds out a collective curse before standing up, where he begins pacing the area behind my desk.

"What are these women being used for, Son?" Pops stops long enough to ask me this before he continues wearing a hole in my flooring.

"Involuntary mates," I answer to another string of curses coming from Pops. "They're kidnapping these women, then auctioning them off to be turned and bred."

"And Anston knows about this?" The look in my pops' eyes as he asks this has me hesitating in answering.

"He's actually one of their financial backers," Kane answers on my behalf, knowing how hard this is on me.

"One of them? There are more?" Pops flops back into his seat, head down in what appears to be shame. I can't let him take this on as a guilt he should carry. It's not his burden to bear, it's these shifters who've violated our laws and ethics.

"Pops, don't…" I don't get to finish before he's waving me away, hands held high in the air as he's angrily swatting them around. If I didn't know any better, I'd swear he was trying to get rid of an annoying fly or gnat. In any other circumstance, I'd be chuckling at his unusual display of annoyance. Pops has always been able to hold his emotions closely guarded inside of himself, so these are unusual gestures for me; I don't know how to react or the right words to say to get him to settle down.

"Who else?" Pops demands. The three of us look at each other, knowing that he's going to flip his shit… all of the men funding this are shifters. Ones we helped get elected to office, ones my father has relations with one way or another.

Ultimately, I'm the one to answer his question. "Jason Glemson and Markus Carmichael."

"No *fucking* way! You've got to be shitting me. This has to be some fucking nightmare that I can't seem to wake from," Pops shouts; his leopard is trying to make an outwardly appearance. Pops' nails have become long sharp points, fur has broken out over his arms, and his fangs have elongated in need to puncture something.

"I wish I was, Pops. This is why I called you in, how the fuck do we take them down? They are so politically connected and coveted by our kind, no one's going to take word of mouth seriously. Even with all the intel we have; it potentially won't be believed. How do I handle this and keep the club safe and clear from gaining unwanted enemies?"

"Jake Broker," Pops announces, catching me off guard.

"The FBI guy?" I question not only his words, but his sanity at this point. We can't let humans get involved in shifter take downs. It would agitate our already shaken point of views on humans. Shifters have always been wary of the intentions humans would have, if they were to ever discover us and our existence. We know they'd want to use us for scientific experimentation and possibly exploit us during times of war. We are all unbelievably strong, heal quick, and have additional abilities that could help the military branches. Our capability of hearing and smelling things that mere humans can't would be useful to the military, and there's no way I want my shifter brethren used in that capacity.

"Yes," Pops hisses out his disdain for my previous words. "That FBI guy, Jake, he's a cougar shifter. He's one of us, Son. He was placed there for times such as this. Although, I have to admit, we never foresaw having to actually use him."

"Shit, Pops. Why didn't I know this?" As the president of this club, I should have all inside knowledge at my disposal.

"You would have, Blaze... eventually. We keep his secret for a reason; when the time was right, I would've told you."

"Well, I guess now is as good of a time as any," Kane states, only his tone is one of frustration and hurt. Secrets like these, if not shared, could be buried with the holder of those facts. Facts, as *president*, I should've been made aware of alongside that of my patched officers. I'm equal parts pissed and hurt that Pops withheld this information from me...from us.

"Jake's been undercover, it wasn't safe for him to be exposed. I need to send him an SOS." Pops grabs his phone and his fingers start to furiously type what I'm presuming is a message to Jake. From the fucking FBI. I wish I'd known that I had a potential helping hand from him the second these women came up missing. I'm a bit perturbed with Pops right now. But we have bigger fish to fry this second, so I'll hold my tongue until there's a better place and time to speak with him about this.

Pops walks out of the room with his phone clutched to his ear once it rings. "Doesn't S.O.S mean shit on the shingles?" Bolt asks. "That's what Mom used to call the biscuits, gravy and sausage mix she used to feed us on the weekends." I see the corner of his lip lift, his tell sign when he's in a joking mood. We could all use a few jokes to ease the tension in the room right now, that's for damn sure.

My face breaks out into a smirk, he knows what it means; he's lightening things up for me, he knows how upset I am right now. And I appreciate it more than words can express. "You know it means 'save our souls'," I continue keeping up the banter.

"Actually," Kane butts in, "it's not an actual acronym for anything. But the ships out at sea use it if they're in trouble. It has also been referenced as 'save our ship'."

"In other words, Pops thinks we're up shit creek without a paddle." And I can't help but agree with his observations. We're in deep shit, and we need a paddle the size of Mount Rushmore to dig our way out of this nightmare of epic proportions.

SEVEN
GLORY

Another day where my eyes stay glued to the auction site. My body shudders as the camera picks up the women in small cages, smaller than a tiny animal should be subjected to. Maritsa's balled up in the cage; there's barely any room for her to switch positions. I can tell by the look on her face that she's in some serious pain. My heart breaks once again for the fact that she's been victimized by my brethren. Being a shifter is a precious gift, one that is sacred and should be treasured by the receiver. We have better senses and are stronger than that of an actual human. But we shouldn't use it to our advantage over those who are physically weaker. We are their protectors; we are meant to look after them and save them from anything supernatural.

Feeling shame for the wrongdoings of others weighs heavily on my chest. For those who grow impatient for their mate to find them, the feeling of loneliness becomes overwhelming; I get that, but that doesn't give anyone the right to snatch someone walking the streets, minding their own business and living their lives.

If you grow tired and restless, I'm of the mindset that you should find yourself a compatible mate. They may not be who the higher powers intend for you, but they'd ease that ache in your chest. But in my personal opinion, some shifters are born evil, filled with a spiteful heart, and don't deserve the peace a mate can bring to you.

Noticing movement on my monitor; I watch as guards enter the room lined with cages. Both men and women are inside of them; we haven't heard of men coming up missing, but clear as day, I can see several.

Opening up my mating link to Blaze, I inform him, *"Women aren't the only victims, my love."*

"Explain, mate. The only missing persons reports we have are that of missing young human females."

"Tell Decoder to show you the site. They have a live, streaming feed of the caged room these individuals are being held in. There are men, Blaze, I'm watching it now and have seen them myself."

"Fuck, I'll get Decoder to bring it to me now. Thanks for the heads up, love, but you shouldn't keep watching this."

"I know, Blaze. But it's like a train wreck in the making. You know you shouldn't be watching, but can't tear your eyes away from it. Tell Dakota, we need to keep this page streaming from our ends. I have a feeling there's something big fixing to happen. They're feeding them and one by one taking them away for periods of time. The ones I've seen come back are clean and in fresh clothes."

"Love, I appreciate the intel, but please stop watching. I worry for your mental well-being. Maritsa is important to your closest friend. And by God, don't let Decoder hear you calling him by his given name. He complains to me about it all the damn time. He's a man now, not a child."

"He was a child whose knees I bandaged when he fell and scraped them. He'll get over it. You call him Decoder, and I will too in front of the brothers, but to me, he'll always be my little buddy and shadow, Dakota."

"Pops has just walked back in the room. I need to speak with him. Love you, Glory girl."

"Love you too, my Blaze of fire."

As my link to him severs, my eyes scan back over to my laptop. "Jesus all mighty," leaves my mouth in a whoosh of air. Maritsa is being dragged from the room; she's stumbling all over the place. They must've drugged her food; she's barely holding herself upright. Calling upon my ancestors, I beg for mercy and guidance for not only myself, but for all of us as we search to find these missing individuals. We are desperately in need of all the assistance and intervention we can get. As I zoom in on the screen, my mouth opens wide.

"Is that?" Oh fuck, no... please no.

BLAZE

"Pops, what was Jake able to tell you?" I ask as soon as he takes a seat at *my* desk. I'm still letting that one go, even though I want to snatch him up and take back my position.

"He wants us to have Decoder send him everything he has. They've had no files of missing people enter their department. No red flags, nothing. He needs Chief Anderson to invite his team in to assist. Legally, from the human aspect of things, illegally... well that's a different story. He'll have to do it on the sly though, he can't let the council catch wind that he's investigating one—several of our own. There are severe consequences into an inquiry of this nature without unwavering substantial proof to support such an accusation as this. He's gonna need to tread lightly, but he's ready and willing to put himself out there, if it means bringing these women home."

"Just spoke with Glory. It's not just women, she's been watching the site for any new movements. Seems as if there's men caged in the same room as the women we know about. I'm not sure how many men, but she was able to see them on the screen. I need to see if Decoder is monitoring it this morning."

"You know he is," Kane rebuts. "He's always watching those screens of his. He's probably trying to figure out who they are before bringing us the information."

As soon as those words leave Kane's mouth, my office door slams open. Decoder and Glory are fighting each other as they both try to enter my office at the same time. "What the fuck? You two know better than to come barging in here without knocking first. I'm in a goddamned private meeting!"

"Pres…"

"Blaze…"

They say, talking over each other. Both look to be out of breath, and Decoder has his laptop snug to his chest. His hands are shaking and Glory's eyes are wide and frantic. "Speak!" I call out, worried about what they are going to share next. Haven't there been enough twist and turns in this horrible situation without adding any more to it? "Decoder?" I look at him, giving him silent permission to speak first. Glory clamps her lips together in irritation. I hide my smirk at the spark of anger she's sending my way.

"Echo," is the only word he stutters out. Echo is my cousin who's been overseas serving our country. He's found a home in the military, and hasn't had any interest in coming back here and joining the MC. My eyes widen and my hand waves in the air, wanting him to continue telling me what's happening with my family. "Echo, he's one of the men being held captive."

"He *what*?" Pops shouts as he forcefully stands up, shooting my chair backward as it goes flying into the wall behind my desk.

My body begins to vibrate with uncontrollable anger and anguish that's streaming through my system. "How? How could they have gotten their hands on him while he's across the goddamned ocean?" My body begins to levitate, my feet leaving the ground, as the reality begins crashing over me. I've always been able to control my abilities, but in times such as this, I have a hard time keeping it reigned in. "Someone better start fucking talking!"

"Once I saw him this morning, I started working on that." Decoder begins speaking rapidly, stating, "It seems he was trying to surprise everyone. He didn't reenlist as we had presumed. He was on his way home to take his place in the MC and family. He was captured somewhere on his route home. His bike is missing. It hasn't been reported as lost or stolen in any of the databases. Somebody knew he was headed home and my guess is, they set up a trap or roadblock to capture him. He wouldn't have willingly gone with them without putting up a struggle. Do you think they somehow drugged him?"

"Who would he have told if not us? At this point, anything is possible." Thinking about this question, I say it out loud unintentionally. I'm trying to put together the pieces of this missing puzzle piece. Why wouldn't he have told me he was coming home? I would've given him an MC escort... hell, I'd have personally gone and rode home with him.

"Anston," Pops blurts out. "He'd have informed Anston to ensure his way through other shifters' territories. He'd have also asked him to keep his return on the downlow to surprise us."

"Fucking Greyhorse is gonna die!" I yell out, blistering my throat from the impact of my screamed declaration. Glory rushes over to me, wrapping her arms around my waist. She has a soothing tone in her voice, but the blood is rushing through my ears and I can't decipher what it is she's saying. Slowly, I feel my body lower back to the ground. Pulling her into my arms, I bury my head in her neck. Her scent is enveloping me, my anger begins to subside from her loving manner. "This can't be happening, Glory," I insist as her arms tighten around me. "It just can't."

"We'll fix it, Blaze. We'll bring him home along with all of the other victims," she declares. And for some reason, her words calm my erratically beating heart and my synapses snap back online and begin to refocus.

EIGHT
BLAZE

Jake called, asking permission to come to our territory for a visit. We granted his wish and he's due to be here any second now. I had a rough night last night after learning Echo was in the clutches of these monsters.

I kept envisioning him being tortured and sold for breeding. But what boggles my mind is that he's a shifter; not a purebred human to be turned. What caused them to change courses? It goes against what they've been doing up to now.

Something had to have changed for them to grab Echo the way they did.

That's the part that we need to figure out. Have they been taking shifters and us... hell, nobody noticed this entire time? Or is this a new development that we only found out with Glory and Decoder seeing Echo with their own eyes?

There's something not computing with this, if they've been going after shifters, why have none been reported as missing? As well as the human men? There has to be people out there missing these loved ones, you'd think.

I'd scour the earth starting a riot of epic proportions if these were my sons, brothers, nephews and uncles.

And that is primarily what I'm not able to comprehend. Shifters are close with their families; their clan, pride or whatever would've taken notice and informed the proper authorities of their missing member.

Going to my humidifier, I pull out one of my cigars. Sitting behind my desk, I prop my feet up on top of it and lean back in my chair. All of the reasons for this are whirling around, causing me to become even more confused as they begin to penetrate. Hopefully, Pops, Jake, Kane, Bolt, Decoder and I can talk this out and come up with a viable conclusion. Because this is seriously grating on my nerves.

All of the unanswered scenarios and possibilities are endlessly causing me to go stir crazy.

Knocking first, Bolt and Kane open the door and come inside. "You look like shit, Blaze," Bolt states. "Didn't sleep?"

"Sure the fuck didn't," I respond, knowing if I look anything like what I feel, his observations are correct.

"It seems as if that's going around," Kane states, lifting the biggest coffee mug I've ever seen and drinking out of it. I'm not sure that it's coffee however, I've never personally witnessed him at the coffee pot. Either way, it's none of my business and I like to keep my nose out of my men's personal lives, unless it interferes with the club. I pride myself in always being there for my men, but never messing around with their ways of coping and managing themselves. I hate assholes who try to nose their way into mine, so I'd never do that to them.

"Pops is on his way here with Jake," I announce. "He called last night asking permission to enter our territory and compound. I'm assuming it means he needs more information or has some of his own to share with us."

"Let's hope for the latter," Kane supplies. "We gave him enough information to lead him to the same conclusions we came up with. Let's just hope he has more at his disposal and was able to find these sons-of-bitches."

"I called Chief Anderson this morning as well. He's looking into other missing persons reports to see if there are any individuals that haven't been connected to our own missing people. There's got to be a connection somewhere; something that made them targets. We need to dig and find more. Something's not sitting right in my gut."

"And that's the question of the hour," a man voices as he walks in the door with Pops.

"Jake?" I ask, sticking my hand out to shake his.

"The one and only," he reciprocates and shakes my hand firmly. "I've heard a lot about you from your dad."

"Wish I could say the same about you," I retort, looking over in my Pops' direction. He shakes his head at me, then turns back to the room.

"If the timing was right, you'd have already met me. I've just wrapped up an undercover operation that I'd been invested in for four years. I couldn't come and make introductions before now. Surely, you understand that." Jake intently holds my gaze without releasing my hand.

"Surely," I mock, still thinking that I should've at least known and been privy to his existence in the first damn place. How am I expected to lead my men to the best of my abilities if I'm not aware of our allies in order to be able to use all the disposable resources I can? After all, that's what a good, dependable leader does.

"Can we stop with the whole whose dick is bigger than whose and figure this shit out already?" Kane admonishes the two of us.

I already know whose is bigger... mine, my leopard announces with pride inside of my mind.

Shush, I silently scold him.

Jake looks away from our gaze and nods his head in Kane's direction. "Good, I'm ready to put a motherfucking hurting on these fuckers and get these men and women home to their families."

"We can all agree on that one," Pops asserts. "Some of them have been missing for several months now, there's no telling what kind of mental and physical trauma they've sustained."

"May I have a seat?" Jake asks, pointing at a chair in the corner of the room. It has a small side table that I'm assuming he wants to use to set his bag on.

"Make yourself at home, Jake." I go for politeness, because my feelings have no merit when it comes to sharing important information.

Everyone's right, the only thing that matters is getting all of these people home and the assholes eliminated and shut down. We need to indict these people for war crimes, because that's exactly what they've done. I will lobby this until I take my last, deathbed breath. I will never stop, never give up, until I've been granted this.

"Decoder gave me some pretty impressive breadcrumbs to follow. I've been able to trace it to the same individuals as he was able to. Here's the issue, the council will come back swinging. They covet all of their members; they'll never believe Anston is capable of such outlandish behavior. We need to basically catch him in the act if we want them on our side," Jake informs us. "It's not impossible, but it's going to be difficult. From what I've been able to decipher, he's not hands on with any of the men and women. The only trace we can tie him to is that of financial backing."

"So, we need to catch him in the act, but how? He's too smart to be caught off guard," Kane says as he leans forward, placing his elbows on his knees. He's running his hands over his head, his forehead wrinkling as he concentrates on his imposing thoughts.

"Pops," Bolt states, "we'll have to use him and his friendship with Anston. If anyone can get him to break, it'd be Pops."

"Pops is retired, we can't ask him to place himself in danger for the club," I remind him.

"Pops is sitting right here, and stop making me refer to myself in the third person, it's fucking humiliating."

"Sorry, Pops," Bolt and I utter at the same time, both of us feeling shame for not including him in our conversation with one another.

"But, I have to agree with Bolt," Pops announces, "out of all of us, I'd be the one he'd trust and possibly slip out something to."

"We have to use all of our resources, Blaze," Kane remorsefully states. "It is the only thing we have at our disposal right now." Fuck, I hate it when he's all logical and shit.

"Pops? Ma's gonna have a damn stroke," I state, feeling bad that my ma will be put through these paces. She was finally feeling settled and at peace with their retirement from all things club related.

"Son, I learned a long time ago that your ma doesn't have to be in the know about everything I do. It keeps her in a happy little bubble. It's my job to keep that from popping. Understand?"

"Sure, Pops. But I'm just putting this out there, if she ever, and I do mean *ever* finds out about this, I'm blaming you on keeping it from her," I deadpan, meaning every damn word because my ma mad, is something I have always preferred to steer clear of. No one can give you a look and words from a sharp tongue and make you feel as low as the dirt buried beneath the grass. She doesn't need to place one finger on me to put me in my place, begging for forgiveness and admitting to all of my sins.

"Whatever you say, Son." Pops chuckles, but he knows that I will solely point the finger in his direction. I'm not above throwing Pops under the bus.

GLORY

I sit next to Dakota watching the live bidding. One girl just went for five hundred thousand dollars and I'm panicking, because neither mine nor the club's offer was accepted on Maritsa. Which means, they believe that they can get more money for her. "Not many shifters have this kind of money sitting aside, Dakota," I cry as I watch the numbers skyrocket for this man who's up right now.

"*Decoder*, Glory. And, they're only selling to people who stand a lot to lose. Not only are these rich motherfuckers; they're also ones who hold positions of power."

"How do you know that?" I ask him, to which he simply raises his eyebrows at me. "Yeah, yeah, I know, you can find anything. But when have you had the time to search?"

"What do you think I've been doing over here while you're watching that?" He points at a secondary computer sitting off to the side. "It's how I multi-task, I can have several windows opened on different systems. This way, nothing ever gets overlooked. I'm following the bidders' IP addresses as they place their bids. They have more money than they know what to do with and need something to spend it on."

"These are living, breathing people, *Decoder*! Not some antique piece up on the auction block."

"Yeah, and most of them don't have a mate or trophy wife to hold down the home front and escort them to charity events. They need someone they can mold and scare into the perfect specimen. I'm not saying it's right, I'm just stating the facts and the way these folks think. I don't agree with their methods, but they have positions and need to show that they are family-oriented people. It'll keep them in good standing within their communities with those who've elected them into their positions of power. It's in their best interest to be viewed, and perceived, as irrevocably dedicated husbands and fathers."

"By inventing their own versions of a Stepford wife," I mumble out.

Thinking about what all that entails makes my stomach violently roll. It means that they'll be brainwashed, hidden and tortured, until they give in and become the most compliant female or male companion.

"First round of auctions is over; we need to figure out who's purchased whom so we can stop them in route." Decoder picks up his phone and calls Blaze. Why he isn't using his mental link with Blaze I don't understand… it'd be so much quicker if he did. "Blaze, first rounds are complete. The ones who've been auctioned off will be leaving with their new owners."

I block out the conversation he's holding with Blaze and lose myself in thoughts. There has to be more we can do to make sure rounds two and three don't come to fruition.

I do manage to overhear and catch the key words as they talk. *In our town,* and *traced it to the old McCrumb factory.* They've been under our noses the entire time and we just now figured it out.

I hope Blaze and the brothers turn them all into ash.

NINE
BLAZE

After getting off the line with Decoder, I pick up the phone and give the coordinates of the auction to Chief Anderson. He's been sitting in wait for us to call so he can set up roadblocks from all exit points from the warehouse where it's being held.

These dumb fucks actually thought they could do this in my town and escape unnoticed? They must think we're a bunch of naïve and stupid assholes. Either that, or they want us to catch them... and that can't be a good thing.

"What if them doing this in our town is a set up?" I ask the men surrounding me. "What if they want us to catch them?"

"What could they accomplish from that?" Kane asks in contemplation.

"To take us out; we're the only threat they really have left. They've got insiders that are pretty high up in both shifter and human government. If the Dark Leopards are taken out, there's nothing holding them back," Bolt insinuates.

"Which is why they took Echo. They wanted to entice us to come to them," Pops states and suddenly it all clicks into place.

Motherfucking, cocksuckers, pieces of shit.

"Did I just send the Chief and his men into an ambush?" Picking my phone back up, I shoot off a text to him letting him in on our suspicions. It's the best I can do, hopefully he receives it before we have a chance to get there and intercept him and his men. "He's not answering my message, we need to go help. If we set him up unintentionally or not, it's our job to provide and offer extra security. Gather the men up, we ride out in three minutes." I watch as both Bolt and Kane pick up their phones and initiate the phone tree we have in place. They'll begin it and each man they contact, will hit the man beneath them.

We arrive at the warehouse fifteen minutes from my first call to the Chief. His men and he have spread out to block all incoming and outgoing roads.

"Just got your message," he says as I climb off my bike and walk up to him. "You think we're in for some trouble?"

"We do," I answer, "so we wanted to be here to assist in case our hunch was correct. My brothers will fan out and help your men wherever they're needed."

"We'll never turn down assistance from you all; place your brothers where you think they'll be the most helpful. I'm gonna go to my car and announce it to my officers." He turns around on the heel of his foot and takes off for his cruiser.

"This ends tonight," I say quietly to Kane. "Place the boys where they'll be the most valuable. No matter what, we leave with all of these men and women alive and in one piece. The bear, lion, wolf and snake must be destroyed. We'll take the others that we know about down differently." My decree is met with a nod of Kane's head.

"Anston, Jason and Markus will be running scared once we chop the head off of their operation," Kane snickers. "I'd love to be a fly on the wall once they discover their money's gone down the drain."

"I've got my men in place to capture the three of them. We need to just worry about getting these people to safety," Jake sneaks up on us and says. He's like a motherfucking ghost; never even heard him approaching.

"Then they're no longer our problem," I state, as Kane takes off to place our brothers where they'll be needed. "We need to get the humans out of here as quickly as possible. They'll be desperate and will most likely shift. We'll have to fight them in animal form."

"I'll take care of that once they escort the survivors out of here and are all out of harm's way," Jake says, then he too walks away and speaks quietly with Chief Anderson.

"Ready or not, motherfuckers, we're coming for you," I declare as my sight zeroes in on the warehouse. My vision is enhanced due to my shifter ability, so I can see our target clearly, whereas the cops are having to use binoculars.

Once everyone is in their allotted positions, Chief Anderson hollers out, "They're moving," and my leopard fights for the rights to own my skin.

"*Not yet*," I mentally converse with him.

"*They hurt our mate, I demand justice and vengeance,*" he engages and sends me a mental picture of his fur standing on end with his fangs elongated.

"And it will be ours, but first we need to get as many humans away and to safety before we go ripping throats out," I try to reassure him that we're on the same damn page.

"As long as I get to kill them—I'll wait," he eventually states. *"But not too long, Blaze."*

"Your leopard demanding blood?" Kane breaks in, causing me to sever my link with my animal.

"Yeah, he's not happy that Glory's been sad and worried. He's clawing my insides wanting to take control. I'm having to talk him off the ledge. He's sequestered himself for now, but he's not promising me he'll allow me to stay in charge for long though."

"My cat isn't happy either, he's ready to rip some damn throats out and is eager for the taste of blood on his tongue." Kane closes his eyes; I'm assuming he's struggling to maintain control over his own skin. When his eyes pop open, I clearly see his cat's eyes. They are sharing his body, both of them present.

"Put your shades on, Kane. We can't afford for the humans to see the way your eyes just changed," I order him. He reaches into his pocket and pulls out his wraparounds, the lenses shaded nearly black. They're the ones that he uses while riding to prevent the sun from glaring in his eyes from the rays reflecting off the pavement.

We crouch down behind some shrubbery waiting for the cars to begin passing. Bolt is further down the road with the others. The men stationed furthest away will grab the first car that leaves and it'll trickle down the line. We'll be grabbing the last car and then infiltrating the old abandoned factory warehouse.

GLORY

Dakota... I mean, Decoder, I have to remember to refer to him by his road name. It's hard for me to decipher between the man he's become and the child I once cared for. He's tapped into the security cameras surrounding the warehouse. It's his way of helping the men prepare for any outside threats that they can't see or hear. I begin relentlessly pacing his room, keeping his monitors within my sights at all times. I have some energy that needs releasing, my leopard isn't happy to be sitting on the sidelines.

"We should be there when they find Maritsa. She knows us and won't be scared if we're there," she hisses at me.

"We'd be placing our mate in danger if we were there, you wench," I hiss back.

"How?" she questions me in a haughty tone.

"Because Blaze would be so intently watching us, worried for us and our safety that he wouldn't be able to concentrate on

himself. Do you want to be responsible if he gets hurt, or worse, killed? It's not worth it, we have to trust in him to get her home safely." Can't get more logical than that with her, she needs to settle herself down and think this through. She's always been more of a leader than a follower. But this time, she needs to sit back and let our man take care of this.

"I'd never do anything to cause our mate harm, Glory!" she pissingly roars at me.

"Then act like it and let me be. I need to concentrate on any outside threats and I can't do that if I'm talking you off the damn ledge!" I holler back out at her and sever our link.

Fucking bitch is relentless.

I'll have to let her shed my skin later this evening and go for a run on the acreage that's surrounding the clubhouse.

"There's activity surrounding the warehouse, Blaze," Decoder says into the intercom. "Two o'clock, snipers up top." It's driving me mad that I can't hear Blaze's responses. My ears prickle as I try to hear, but the earpiece is tucked into Decoder's ear.

"Fucking hell, give me one of those," I demand as I point at his ear.

He hesitantly looks over at me before stating, "I'll give you an earpiece, but not a mic. Blaze cannot afford to hear your voice right now. It'll break his concentration. Deal?"

"Whatever, as long as I can hear his voice, my animal and I will settle down," I admit.

He leans over and pulls open a drawer. Disabling the microphone, he hands it over to me. "It's already Bluetoothed in, you'll be able to hear everything I do." I nod my head then reach over and grab the earpiece from his outstretched hand. Slipping the tiny piece inside of my ear, I listen to the activity as I watch it stream live, in real time in front of me.

I silently watch as each car is stopped, and victim after victim is hauled away in an unmarked van. There's also a van that's taking the cuffed drivers and bidders away. Then, as if my life is flashing in front of my eyes, bullets begin peppering at our men as the sniper Decoder warned Blaze about begins targeting them.

"No," I stammer out, throwing my hands over my eyes. I can hear everything happening, but I feel as if I'm not watching it, it's not really happening.

Unfortunately, that couldn't be further from the truth.

TEN
BLAZE

"Take cover!" I yell out, we can recover from a nick, but no one can come back from a fatal wound... not even shifters.

We can die just like most humans... car wrecks, knife stabs, falling off a cliff. It's all a possibility in the realm of things; we can shift and heal bruises, scrapes and broken bones, but we aren't exceptions to all. Most of the time shifters feel invincible, so we have to keep in mind that we are sometimes vulnerable as well.

As a bullet whizzes by the top of my head, my leopard begins to shed my skin. My hands and arms begin sprouting fur. When I'm in mortal danger, it's his job to come out and protect me. Knowing all the humans are busy protecting their lives and not watching me, I allow him to take control. As my bones break and reform, I give myself wholly over to my leopard. My claws begin to form and I hunch over as my clothes begin to shred. Looking down, my hands are now that of paws. My leopard is as white as the driven snow with pale black and grey splotches. My eyes sharpen and my ears perk up; taking in all of the noises surrounding me.

"Shift, it's time to take out the trash," I order my men through our mental link. *"Just don't let the humans see you doing it."*

"They're all hiding and can't see us," Bolt responds to me.

"Let's take them out, I'm tired of fucking around with these pussies," Kane hisses through the link. All of my men agree and I can feel the power surging around me as we all take on the form of our predators. It's time to go hunting!

As a finely tuned group, we all take up surrounding areas. We break apart, some going North, some going South, while the rest of us take vigil at the front and back.

"Decoder?" I call his name through the pride link.

"I'm here," he replies.

"We need to get these human officers out of here, Decoder, can't have any casualties or fatalities."

"The best I can do is call them back. You know Chief Anderson's not going to leave until everyone is safe and accounted for," he responds. "I'm calling him now, hopefully he answers."

"He will if you call from the club's land line," I inform him, knowing that the Chief is aware we have cameras surrounding us.

"10-4," he states before breaking our link. Looking over in the Chief's direction, I see him pull out his phone then answer. His eyes scrunch together as he briefly argues with Decoder before eventually nodding his head.

"The officers and Chief Anderson will be pulling away shortly. Once they do, we'll all charge in," I direct my men and hear all of them acknowledge me. I watch as all of the patrol cars pull away, and then state one word, *"Go!"*

You can hear our paws digging into the grass as we all charge, focused on gaining ground and entering the factory, ducking and weaving bullets as they are directed at our animals. I hear a whine come from one of our men who then states, *"Just a graze, I'm fine."*

No one stops in their pursuits, if someone was seriously injured, and couldn't heal while shifted, they'd tell me and I'd send them back to recover and be treated.

Gaining ground, my team makes it to the front door, I shift my paw into my hand as I reach up and turn the knob. As alpha, I have the ability to partially shift, my other teams will have to have a member shift back into his human skin and open the back door for them. The ones taking up residence at the sides of the building will capture and detain anyone who tries to sneak out. Jake has joined us; even though he isn't able to speak with us through our shared link, he's just taking cues from our team.

As I pull the door open, all of the cats go down on their front paws with their rear ends sticking up. It's our prowling stance, one we only use when we're going after a target. As the door bangs open, I shift my hand back into my paw and lead the charge into the warehouse.

The inside is full of activity as guards rush to secure their prisoners and fight for their freedom. Something they won't be receiving; my men will ensure and see to that.

I set my eyes on the wolf that's sneaking around all of the men fighting. Running full speed, I jump on his back and place my fangs at his jugular. He tries to buck me off, but my claws bury themselves into his skin. He has become my captive, he tries to flip us to where I'm on my back, putting me at a disadvantage. My back legs wrap around his hips, he struggles against my tight hold. I hear him growl in frustration as his lack of movement is pissing him off. I can feel it in the air and internally smile at his forlorn predicament.

His life will be mine, I think as my fangs further penetrate his skin. The taste of fur and blood enrapture my senses and I feel victory on the horizon. *Mine.*

His body shudders beneath me as his life force drains from his shifted body. He goes limp underneath me and my cat yowls his victory. I leave my conquest dead on the floor and follow my nose to where it scents my cousin.

I can feel his anxiety which pushes me faster.

Is he hurt?

In trouble?

Has something happened to put him in distress?

I'll kill whoever has made him feel this way. Fear is engulfing my system, I can feel it swarming me, wrapping me in an uncomfortable embrace. My body picks up speed as I come to an opened door leading underground.

We don't have cellars here in Texas. This one doesn't carry the odor of an old musky smell; which means it's not old, it's freshly built.

I'm presuming it was dug as an addition; the motherfuckers needing somewhere to store innocent people before they started bringing in their kidnapped individuals. This underground bunker of sorts was a brilliant idea on their part; it has concealed everyone's screams along with their scents of fear and hurt.

Any shifter within a five-mile radius of this place would've been able to notice it. Leaping down the last few stairs, I stop dead in my tracks when I take in the lined cages taking up every square inch of this basement. There's barely a path to walk through, cages are on top of cages, the air is thick and hard to breathe through.

As my eyes scan the room at large, they land on that of my cousin who makes eye contact with me and lets out a ragged breath.

"Thank God you found me," he weakly blurts out. "Get me out of here, Blaze."

I shift back into my human skin and run toward him. There are locks on the cages, but they are nothing compared to my superhuman strength. Hearing footsteps coming down the steps, I lift up my nose and smell. It's my team, my body relaxes as I hear them too begin to break loose the locks.

Kane walks over to me with a fresh set of clothes. He must've gone back to our bikes and retrieved my spare set I keep stored in my saddle bags for instances such as this. Quickly putting them on, I keep my eyes on my cousin, scared that like a mirage he'll disappear in front of my eyes.

"Echo, are you alright?" I ask him as soon as I have dressed and released him from his locked enclosure.

"I'm good, but damn I'm glad to see you." He leans into my body where we embrace each other. "I smell her, Blaze. My mate, she's trapped down here somewhere."

"You don't know who she is?" I ask, leaning him back and watching his eyes as they meticulously look around.

"No, but she's somewhere close," he answers, once again taking in all of the happenings surrounding us.

"Blaze!" I hear a familiar feminine sound call out my name. "Blaze! Help me," the voice cries out.

"Maritsa?" I turn and take in the young woman as she runs and leaps into my arms.

I feel my body jerk as my cousin hisses out, *"Mine."*

Oh fuck! This cannot be happening! Glory will skin him alive if he touches one hair on her head. Maritsa's almost seventeen years old… which means Echo can't claim her until she's turned eighteen. "Echo, she's too young. You can't claim her for another year or so."

His eyes darken as he narrowly looks over at me. "Don't have to claim her to protect her. Still don't want any other man's hands on her. Understand?"

"Undoubtedly," I inform him as I begin sitting Maritsa down. She's already had her life turned upside down, she doesn't need to see a shifter lose his marbles over his future mate, we are known to be uncontrollable and lethal when another person touches what's destined to be ours. "Let's get everyone out of here so that the Chief can make sure everyone gets the medical treatment they need and are returned to their families."

GLORY

Happy tears stream down my face as I watch the monitors and see the kidnapped victims being escorted out of the factory.

They did it!

They saved every last one of them. A gasp leaves my throat when I see Echo carrying Maritsa out. She has her arms wrapped around his neck and his face is buried into the top of her head. When they look at each other, they both bear the look of someone who's found their mates. Am I seeing this wrong? Fucking hell, Angela is going to shit her pants if Echo becomes a permanent figure at their house.

If my assumptions are correct, he won't be able to not keep her in his line of sight. He'll have to be around her to calm the raging beast inside of himself.

Blaze and I didn't even make it a weekend before we had to be in each other's presence. Our families got together and had a quick little claiming ceremony before the clan one. Our bond was sealed before we'd even left each other at the festival. We didn't sink our teeth into one another, nor have any sort of sexual encounter for our bond to seal. We were just around one another, chemistry sparked between us, but we respected our families and the customs enough not to tarnish them.

Looks as if another couple will be having their own soon. In a year or so from now; I hope Angela is ready for the big extended family she'll gain in all of us.

Angela will soon have to be told about us, it's the only way she'll be able to understand the need for our animal to be close to their mate at all times. Otherwise, it'll be agonizing for the both of them. Maritsa may be human, but now that her and Echo's paths have crossed, the mating instincts are already taking hold of them both.

Just because Maritsa isn't a shifter, doesn't mean that she won't feel every ounce of pain that Echo does. It's an immediate link, one that neither one of them will be able to break or severe the ties. Unfortunately, human or not,

Maritsa is about to discover how painful it can be to be separated from her intended, fated mate.

Her limbs are going to seize up, she's going to constantly feel ill to her stomach, there is no saving her from this. As much as I wish I had a magical remedy for her, none exist. Echo will either be a permanent resident at Angela's house, or Maritsa will be living here with her future family.

Either way, we're fixing to expose ourselves to my friend and her daughter. And if I know Angela the way I do, she's gonna freak and try to vanish with her baby girl. Supernatural life is beyond her realm of understanding. To her it's fictionalized in books, she is a sucker for all things shifter related… when it comes to reading about them.

I'm both anxious and excited to see her eyes when she finds out that her favorite reading genre is not a made-up fantasy.

Who knows, maybe she'll surprise me and accept it wholeheartedly and I'll have been worrying about nothing.

Time will soon tell.

ELEVEN
BLAZE

Echo refuses to let go of Maritsa, not that I can actually blame him for this act. But when we get her home to Angela, he's going to have some tough decisions to make. But as always, I will be at his side helping him out any way that I can.

"Maritsa, we need to talk about everything you saw and heard while in captivity," I begin. Her red-rimmed eyes look up at me, removing her head from Echo's shoulder.

"Can you turn into an animal too, Blaze?" she questions me with a wobbly lip. I can see how much all of this is affecting her, and I wish I could fix it for her.

"Yes, Maritsa, I can." My answer has her eyes widening, even though she asked the question and possibly suspected as much, having it confirmed seems to be hard for her to accept.

"And Aunt Glory, can she also change into an animal?"

"Yes, sweetheart. We're both leopards." Throughout the years, I've learned that answering a question such as this needs to be quickly executed. It's like ripping a band aid off quickly so you don't feel the hairs coming off with the sticky ends.

"That's really pretty cool," she says with a bit of awe in her voice. "And you, Echo?" She turns her attention to him, but I can tell she really is hoping he'll say he is.

"I am. I'm also a leopard like Blaze and Glory," he answers. I can see the worry in his eyes, he needs her to accept him and his animal as well.

"Why do I feel so drawn to you, Echo? I've never felt this need to be as close to someone as I do you. Is that normal?" I can see the confusion written on Maritsa's face as she ask him this.

"There's a lot I need to explain to you, Maritsa," Echo informs her. "But we don't have to get into all of that right now. First, we need to get you to your mother. She needs to see with her own eyes that you are safe and alive."

"I can't." she begins to roughly breath, I'm fearful she's fixing to have a panic attack. "You can't leave me!"

"I won't, I swear to you I won't," he soothing states as he pulls her head back into his chest. He looks up at me with wide, fearful eyes. This is new to all of us, no one in our family has been mated to a human and had to explain it to them in full detail. The things she'll be feeling and experiencing are going to make it hard for her to stay away from him, from all of us. She'll need that Familia bond in order to make it through each day.

"I think you should explain it all to her now, brother. She knows about us, it'll be easier for her to understand and comprehend the feelings she's experiencing," I tell Echo.

We pull over to the side of the road and spend the next hour explaining and answering Maritsa. Through our link, I told Glory what was taking place and asked her to meet us at Angela's. We can't put off telling her about us, this, because there's no way Maritsa will make it for any amount of time without Echo by her side.

I just hope Angela is willing to have an open mind. Because if she denies Echo, she could possibly kill her only child. Maritsa will slowly break down, her body will shut itself completely off, and if she dies as a result, so will Echo. And that is something I'll never sit idly by and watch happen.

"We have to explain all of this to your mom, Maritsa. You and Echo cannot be apart for an extended period of time now that y'all have come face-to-face. It can and will destroy you both. Death has been known to occur in these instances."

I don't know this for a fact personally, no one in my family has mated to someone who's non-shifting, but I've read reports of it happening.

"She'll understand, I'll make her," Maritsa strongly declares. "If just the thought alone of Echo leaving is hurting this much; I can't imagine what it'll do to me if he actually leaves."

"She may not take it well, Maritsa. I don't want you giving yourself any false hopes here. I need you to promise me something," I sigh.

"What's that, Blaze?" she asks back.

"If your mother gets inside of her head about all of this and tries to run. Promise me you'll call us first. I can't even begin to explain to you the pain you and Echo will both suffer if you leave. The more distance placed between the two of you, the harder and more painful life will become."

"Wild horses couldn't drag me away! But I do promise; if she reacts badly, and tries anything of the sort, I will call you," Maritsa deadpans.

"That's all we can ask of you, my beautiful mate," Echo purrs.

"Mate. I'm somebody's mate." Maritsa does her own form of purring once she says this out loud.

"Now and forever, my love," Echo responds.

I remember how he's feeling right about now. I just can't believe that he's found his mate and she's so damn young. This is going to be a test of wills for him… for both of them.

Thinking I'm gonna need backup, I text Jake and ask him to meet us there. If things don't go well, he has the resources to get the medication needed to erase Angela's memory.

The only problem with that, is that it'll erase everything, every memory she has of her past. She'll be lost for the rest of her life. And we'll have to stand by on the sidelines and watch as she struggles. I don't know how Maritsa and Glory will deal with that.

GLORY

I nervously stand on Angela's doorstep. My heart is pounding furiously inside of my chest cavern. I don't want to lose my friend, but the possibility is high that once she discovers the truth about me, she'll not only feel hurt and betrayed, but may be disgusted by what I truly am.

I've never come out to someone as a leopard shifter before; my nerves are flying high with apprehension. All of this is important, she can't deny Maritsa and Echo, I cannot let that happen.

"Glory, how long are you going to stand out here on the porch and contemplate knocking?" Angela asks me as she flings open the door and gives me an annoyed look. "Y'all found her didn't you? Oh God, is she…?" She breaks down into tears before finishing that thought.

"She's okay, I swear she is, Angela." I pull my friend into my embrace and comfort her. I'm so mad at myself, my standing here, staring at her door, gave her the wrong impression. "Blaze has her, they'll be here soon."

"Come in, we need to get some food prepared. There's no telling how long it's been since my baby had a good meal," Angela pronounces as she pulls herself away from me.

"Blaze also found his cousin there," I announce, following her into her kitchen.

"How many women did y'all rescue?" she asks, pulling out a loaf of bread then heading for her refrigerator. I watch as she pulls out the makings for a sandwich.

"They didn't just have women, Angela. Blaze's cousin, Echo, was captured on his way home to surprise everyone."

"Oh no!" Her hands come up to cup her mouth and it's then I notice how bad their shaking. "I don't understand any of it, why? Why did they do this to my baby, to the others?"

"There's a lot to explain, a lot I still don't know. It's best if we wait for Blaze and Echo to get here and help us understand," I lie. I'm a damn coward, I need my man to help me get through this conversation.

"Yeah, okay, these sandwiches aren't going to make themselves. Do you suppose that Blaze and, what did you say his name was? Echo? If he was taken too, he's most likely just as starved as my Maritsa. Right?" she stammers, I can tell she's trying to keep herself busy by talking and preparing enough food for everyone.

"I'm sure Echo will be starving." I don't add that a shifter's metabolism makes us ravenous throughout the day. We could eat from the moment our eyes open until they close at the end of each night.

As soon as we have sandwiches, chips and sodas gathered on the table, we hear the unmistakable sound of a vehicle pulling into the driveway.

"Are you ready for this?" I ask Angela as I grab her hand in mine.

"Like you wouldn't believe," she answers as we stand in the mouth of the hallway, anticipating their entrance.

Time feels as if it's standing still as we stand here. I can feel how twitchy Angela is, I know that she wants to run out and pull Maritsa into her arms, but how she also fears overwhelming her. So, she fights herself to keep her feet planted firmly on the ground.

What feels like hours, but is only minutes, Maritsa comes walking into the house, with Echo's hand in hers. They're entering as a united front. A small smile erupts on my face, the corner of my mouth tilts up as I take in how connected the two of them already are.

"Maritsa," Angela whispers as tears stream down her cheeks. "My baby," she chokes out as she spreads her arms wide.

Maritsa tugs Echo with her as she runs into her mother's embrace. It's nearly comical to see this larger than life man, struggling to keep up with his mate.

Angela doesn't seem to notice him, or if she does, she's chosen to ignore the fact that this man, nearly ten years older than her daughter, is glued to the two of them. I watch as Angela's eyes swing to Echo, her eyes widen;

almost as if she recognizes him, before pulling him into their arms.

"Is it me, or do you have the feeling that this is all gonna work out?" Blaze asks me as he comes up behind me and wraps his arms firmly around my middle.

"It seems as if she recognizes him as her family. It's odd, isn't it, Blaze?"

"It's the magic of love and family, Glory," he says as he places an open palm to my stomach where one day, I'll be growing the life that we make together.

TWELVE
BLAZE

I keep Glory tightly wrapped in my arms as we watch this family come together. Angela may not know all of our deepest, darkest secrets, but it appears as if she may have already accepted Echo as one of her own.

The sound of a vehicle approaching has me turning around to look through the picture glass window.

"Who is it, Blaze?" Glory asks me.

"That's Jake. Pops' friend from the FBI," I inform her as I reluctantly let go of her so I can go and open the front door for him. She trails behind me as I pull it open.

"Blaze." Jake sticks out his hand for a shake. "I'm glad you called; these situations can get sticky at times. Better to be prepared ahead of time."

"I can't thank you enough for coming. This is my mate, Glory," I introduce them to one another.

"Nice to meet you, ma'am," Jake politely says, beaming a smile in her direction.

She returns his smile as she shakes his hand. "Jake, won't you come in, please."

"Thank you," he responds, but once he walks inside, he halts his steps and takes a big whiff of the air surrounding us. *Mate*, I hear a rumbled yowl leave his chest. Then a continuous purr begins loudly making itself known.

Glory yanks on my shirt as my head turns in her direction. "Mate," she mouths to me with wide, worried eyes. It seems as if Angela is going to get a double whammy of information overload today. She's going to learn that shifters exist along with finding out she's a life mate to a damn cougar shifter. We may need the largest prescription available of Xanax to help get her through this.

Jake pushes his way around us and goes in search of his eternal mate. I sigh. "Jake, man, remember she's human. She has no clue about our existence."

"Have to find her, I can feel her distress. My cat needs to be the one to comfort her, I can't stop him, Blaze." Jake continues along his path of searching out his heart's deepest desire.

When we walk into the kitchen, Angela is setting a bunch of food on the table. Her back is turned to us, but as soon as Jake's presence is felt by her, her shoulders stiffen as she slowly turns around.

When their eyes connect, Angela's hands begin to quiver. "I know you, I don't know how, but I do," she says with a shaky voice.

"My name is Jake," he tells her as he walks up to her and grabs the bowl filled to the brim with potato chips.

Scanning the room, not wanting to feel as if I'm imposing on their first meeting, I notice Echo and Maritsa at the table watching the interaction between her mother and this newcomer. "Is? Is that what I think it is?" Maritsa asks me.

"Yes, sweet girl, that is your mother's life mate making a connection," I answer her, stumbling over my words.

I hope she's able to accept this for her mother. Her mother has sacrificed everything for her growing up. She never, not once, went on a date, not wanting to tarnish her late husband's memory where her daughter was concerned. She wanted Maritsa to understand that Calvin was the love of her life and something of that magnitude, a love as pure as the one they shared once upon a time; isn't to be taken lightly.

"I'm so happy for her," she whispers quietly, and if I hadn't been the shifter that I am, with extended, supernatural hearing capabilities; I would've completely missed what she said.

GLORY

My eyes bounce back and forth between Echo and Maritsa and Angela and Jake. I knew there was a reason I felt so connected to this mother and daughter duo. It's because they're meant to be one of us, it's that magical string that pulls us to one another. I may not have understood our link to one another in the beginning, but it's all loud and clear for me now. I've witnessed many unions in my lifetime, but none that were so intimately connected to me.

I feel as if the universe pulled us together so that I could be here for the two of them now during this life's transition. I'll be able to answer all of their questions where it pertains to shifters and what they can expect their life to become. Many things will be changing for the two of them.

Their sight will sharpen, as well as their hearing. They'll be much stronger than the average human, things they've struggled with before, will be as easy as snapping their fingers together.

"Shall we eat?" I ask, breaking the tension in the room. Angela's head whips in my direction before mimicking a bobblehead.

"Yeah," she stammers out, taking a quick look up in Jake's direction before sliding around him.

Around the dining room table, everyone's mouths are busy eating, no one says a word as we consume the food. Once everyone is full, I help Angela clear the table and take care of the dishes.

"There's something you're not telling me, isn't there, Glory?" she asks me as she dries a plate.

"There is, but wait until we're done and we'll all sit down to chat," I attempt to dismiss the conversation. Not wanting to be alone while the cat is let out of the bag… no pun intended.

I hand her the last glass, and as she finishes drying it, she gives me a side glance before heading off toward the living room. I sigh with dread, not sure if it's because

I'm fearful of the way she'll take the news, or worried that she'll try to run off in the dead of the night.

Not that Jake nor Echo will make that easy on her. I have a feeling they'll both be camping outside of her home tonight… and many nights to come until she fully accepts them into her life. But who knows, she may surprise me. Stranger things have happened. It's the fear of the unknown that has me all boggled up inside.

I'm still standing there in front of the sink when Blaze comes strolling in. "We can't put this off forever, Glory. Come on," he imparts as he sticks his hand out for me.

"We can try," I mumble underneath my breath. "Can't Jake just change her so she doesn't have a choice?" I hopefully ask, because that would be much easier on me in the long run.

"And take away her free will? That's not the way things work and you know it, Glory." Why does he have to go and be all sensible and shit?

"I suppose," I once again sigh, wanting to drag my feet for as long as he'll allow me to.

"I've got you, Glory."

I snap my shoulders into an upright position before we make our way in, joining the others. I need to be strong for my friend, not the coward I'm currently being. This is about her at the end of the day, not me.

THIRTEEN
GLORY

"All right, we've eaten and stalled, now someone start talking," Angela says, taking the lead. Jake is hovering at her side; I can feel fear in waves as he suddenly acts as if he's got a dry mouth. Shouldn't he be the one leading this conversation? I would think that'd be the case since things have flipped and it's he who needs to gather the courage and explain this shit to his future mate.

Am I right? I don't know, but it's how I'm feeling anyway. I turn in Jake's direction and widen my eyes at him. I'm trying to portray to him to get his ass in gear. He gives me a look of utter devastation before he gathers his composure and ends up in front of Angela. He gets down on his knees so that he can be eye level with her.

"Angela, this is going to sound like some sort of fairytale, but please let me explain everything before you react," Jake tells her as he takes her hand in his.

"I'll do the best that I can," she promises. She's not the best at not breaking into an explanation without asking many, many questions.

"There are supernatural beings that live in harmony with humans." Oh dear lord, I roll my eyes at how he starts this thing. He clears his throat then continues, "Do you believe that that is a possibility?"

"If you mean, do I believe in aliens like ET living amongst us, pretending to be humans, no, I don't. Now, if you're asking me if I believe that shifters exist, then the answer is yes." My ears prickle when she states this.

"What do you know about shifters?" I ask her, curious about why she'd say what she just did.

"Calvin was a keeper of many secrets, Glory. But you know he kept nothing from me," Angela explains.

"Can you expand on that, please?" Blaze queries.

"Calvin's family was one of the entrusted humans to keep shifter secrets. He helped protect your kind on several occasions," she explains.

"Um, our kind?" I hesitantly examine her statement.

"Yes, Glory, your kind. Why do you think I didn't probe into the way your eyes would change color if your emotions were at an all-time high? The way your fingernails would miraculously extend, or your voice would change tones all of a sudden? There are those of us who've taken an oath to protect you guys at all cost. I've extended Calvin's vow on as my own when he passed."

"Why didn't you ever say anything to me?" I can't help but wonder.

"Because, Glory, how would I be protecting your secret and Calvin's family if I blurted that out to you? It's supposed to be a secret, but I have this feeling that this is what you were about to share with me. Is that right, Jake?"

"Yeah," he skeptically answers her. "It is."

"Mom?" Maritsa butts in, "how much do you know about mates among the shifter kind?" Angela's eyes widen as her daughter asks this of her.

"Only what your father shared with me, Maritsa," Angela answers as she closes her eyes. "Why do you ask?"

"Because, I'm Echo's mate," Maritsa shyly reports.

"You're only sixteen!" Angela shouts out. "You can't mate with him, you have to be of age to consent, and I'm not letting this happen! Not yet anyway."

"I would never disrespect Maritsa or you in that manner," Echo vehemently denies. "I want to take the time until she comes of age to get to know her and you. You two are my family, all I ask is that you allow me to be around."

"That, I can work with," Angela deflates as she speaks this. "You will always be welcome in our home, Echo."

"I appreciate that, thank you," Echo returns.

BLAZE

It's not every day that you find out that your tightly held secret isn't as hush-hush as you believed it to be. I'm still quite stunned as I stand back and witness this family begin their journey of bonding.

Jake begins to fidget as he decides on the best way to inform Angela that she too, is a mate to a shifter. His mate. He needs to find his balls and quickly tell her this, she's all open and willing to hear all that we have to share.

I think that the information he's withholding is prudent to her future. She'll be pissed off if it hits her harder in the face without her understanding what all it is she's feeling where it pertains to him.

"Jake," I say his name, trying to push him into confessing.

"Angela," he says her name, but his eyes are shifting around the room, I can feel the nervous energy coming from him in waves. It's almost enough to cause my heart to leap from my chest.

"Tell me," she whispers as she too begins to restlessly move around. Shifting from hip to hip on the couch.

"Angela, you are my mate," Jake finally spits out.

"I know, Jake, I felt it the moment you came into the kitchen. I was just waiting for you to confirm my beliefs."

"You did?" Jake asks her.

"I did. I wasn't sure at first what that emotion was that was strumming through me. Why I felt this invisible string pulling me toward you. Then, it dawned on me when I looked up and noticed you were looking at me the same way Blaze looks at Glory. Full of love and admiration. I'm not saying you're in love with me, I'm just saying that's the way it felt. I mean, it's too soon for love," she continues stammering out her words.

"Angela," Glory calls out to her friend, "just breath, sweetheart, it's all going to be okay. You can feel the way you want to. This is your life, and if you recognize the bond, then it's a true match."

"I concur with my mate." I think things over before I articulate my advice, "there's no right or wrong way to understand and comprehend your feelings. Finding one's life mate is magical, there isn't one way to handle these things, it's not textbook. Everyone handles and does things differently. Just breathe, Angela, we've got you."

"Getting to know you, I can do that," Angela finally concurs.

Glory and I stick around a little longer, acting as a buffer between the four of them. When we're both satisfied, we bid everyone our farewells, but not before Jake has the opportunity to pull me off to the side.

"Your Chief Anderson, he took the men that were left alive and has taken them to the human jail."

"Which means the council is going to find out about our little showdown and rescue mission." I think out loud, knowing that life is fixing to get a lot more interesting in my little neck of the woods. "We should've killed them all."

"Maybe, but this may work to our advantage, Blaze."

"How do you figure?" I ask him, not understanding where he's coming from.

"This means that Greyhorse and the other two are going to be scrambling, trying to cover their tracks," he slowly says as things start to sink in.

Then, as if a lightbulb has gone off over my head, I get it. "If we're monitoring their activity, we're bound to find enough information to take them down."

"My thoughts precisely, they'll make a mistake trying to bury evidence, and we, my friend, will be there to intercept the files before they get lost in cyber space."

"And at least that way, Pops won't have to subject himself to a face-to-face meeting with his friend."

"He'll be able to honestly say that he didn't betray their long-standing friendship," Jake concurs.

"I'll get Decoder on it," I inform him.

"And I'll have my man assisting. I'll make sure he's available to aid Decoder any way possible," Jake imparts as he slaps me on the shoulder then heads off to his mate.

I go in search of my own. I'm ready to get home. My leopard wants to shift and run with his mate. And I'm obliged to give him his way.

FOURTEEN
BLAZE

We held a quick church session this morning. I advised everyone of what was going down. Decoder is already working on some code thing that will automatically copy files the three fuckfaces try to erase and bury. We also decided to host a barbeque for the two newest couples in our midst. It's times like this that we need to celebrate the good things in life.

As soon as Glory heard we wanted to rejoice in her friend's honor, she got down to business and is planning the menu. Pops called last night as soon as Glory and I got done letting our cats run and play and informed me that he broke down and told Ma about Greyhorse. Needless to say, she was shocked and ultimately cried herself to sleep. Betrayal by someone you consider family is a hard pill to swallow.

Pops was choked up while speaking with me, which makes me that much more determined to make Greyhorse pay for his crimes against humanity and our kind.

Jake and Echo have chosen to stay with Angela and Maritsa, for the time being at least. No one knows how this is going to play out, and neither one of them want to leave their mate unguarded and vulnerable.

I pick up the phone and give Echo a call. His phone goes straight to voicemail before I remember that his phone and belongings were found with his bike. One of my men went venturing out after the attack that saved and rescued men and women, and eventually found it hidden under some brush. I was given his things this morning and need to return them to him as well as his bike. It has some bumps and bruises, but nothing that can't be fixed.

Deciding there's no time like the present, I grab his keys and belongings, stuffing them in his saddlebags before heading off in his direction. I fire up his bike and a smile grows on my face as I hear this bad boy purr to life.

The gas tank is painted in camo green and brown, which is why it blended so seamlessly in with the leaves and branches without being spotted easily. I lovingly pat it as one would their child and hit the road.

I enjoy the short ride, the wind in my hair always has a calming effect on me and my leopard.

When I pull up into Angela's driveway, Echo comes outside. He has a smile on his face that stretches from one ear to the other.

"You found her!" he excitedly exclaims as he heads over to check on his beloved bike.

"We did, she was hidden, but isn't in too bad of shape," I gleefully respond.

"I don't know how to thank you, Blaze. For everything," he declares as he runs his hands through his once military shaved head, that has now grown past his ears. I don't know why I notice this detail, but I haven't seen him with anything but a military cut since he joined the armed forces.

I think it's because I've decided to notice and enjoy everything around me. You can't take life for granted and we need to relish the little things in life. You never know what tomorrow might bring.

"There's no reason to thank me, Echo, we're not just brothers, we're blood," I state, sticking out my hand for a shake. He simply shakes his head at me as he pulls me into his embrace. He slaps me on the back before pulling away.

"Jake and Angela jumped the gun last night," he informs me. "She was well claimed if the noises I heard last night are any indication. She'll be needing to shift soon."

We usually shift within twelve hours of our body's transformation. It takes that long for our cells to regenerate to that of our animal. Her first change is going to be very painful, and she'll need others around her to help soothe the beast inside.

"We're having a barbeque tonight, you four are our guests of honor. Why don't you go get Jake up and moving and get Angela to the compound. It'll be the best place for her to be for her first shift," I advise, using my alpha voice. This is our friend; I want to be there and help her and Jake through this. It'll end up being just as painful for him as it will be for her. He'll feel every break of her bones and every tear that trails down her face.

That bond cannot be helped, we experience everything that our mates do. It's nature's way of keeping us united.

"How are you going to get back?" Echo asks me.

"My four paws," I inform him as I walk across from Angela's house and into the woods that lead to our backyard.

"See ya soon," he hollers out to my retreating back. I wave over my head but am anxious to get back to Glory.

There was something off about my woman this morning. Her scent changed overnight. And if it's what I suspect it is, I can't wait to embrace the news and make love to her until it's time to gather with our friends and family.

GLORY

When a shifter conceives, it's an instantaneous knowledge the next morning after conception. Not only can you feel the difference in your body, but you can sense the life growing inside of you. Last night did it for Blaze and me, our round of lovemaking in the woods after letting our animals free, we were given the ultimate gift. The gift of new life.

I'm not sure if Blaze noticed the difference in me this morning, but he raised an eyebrow at me as we ate breakfast. But he had a church meeting planned and couldn't stick around to grill me about the change.

Tonight, I'll tell him at the barbeque. There's no better time than to inform him of his impending fatherhood than where he can embrace that with his family at our side.

I can't believe my dream is finally coming true. I've always dreamed of the day that I would become a mother. When Blaze told me he was ready to start trying, I had no idea it would happen as quickly as it did.

As I stand over the stove, mashing potatoes, my hand goes down and lovingly caresses my belly where my baby is peacefully growing.

"I can't wait to meet you," I impart to my child. "You're going to become the most loved baby on the planet."

The party is in full swing, everyone is enjoying the fruits of my labor and I couldn't be any happier than I am at this moment.

Angela had her first shift earlier this evening, it was painful to watch her struggle the way she did. Her body was fighting the change, we all had to shift in order to ease her into it. Eventually it worked, and she's the most magnificent cougar I've ever encountered.

"I have a few words I'd like to say," Blaze states into the microphone we set up. I knew he'd have some words to share, and I was right. "Tonight, we're not only celebrating two of our own finding their mates, but we celebrate life!" Everyone applauds him and he lifts his arms up to quiet them. "We not only rescued and saved the lives of many, but two of our own were captured and ultimately united. Angela, Maritsa, welcome to the family, ladies."

Angela and Maritsa are swarmed with hugs and warmly accepted words. Both of them look happy as their mates hold them in their arms. Echo is being very gentlemanly and is being a man of his words. A little touch here, a hug there, this is actually the most intimate I've seen him with her.

I'm proud of the man he is and that he's waiting and not pushing things with Maritsa. She's still young and has so much life to experience. He'll just go on the path of growth with her. He'll get to experience and witness a lot of her firsts as she becomes a woman.

Before Blaze gets the chance to step down, I go up and join him on the platformed stage the men constructed earlier for me.

Grabbing the microphone from him, I inform him, "I have something I'd like to say if you don't mind."

"Our first lady has something she'd like to say, everyone quiet down," Blaze roars into the night air. Everyone stills and sends their attention in my direction.

"Thank you," I begin, "first, I want to tell you all how much Blaze and I love you. This is the best family a woman could wish to be part of. When I first came here, you all embraced me with open arms, never making me feel like I was an outsider who needed to prove myself to you all in order to claim my position at Blaze's side. Second, I want to tell you all," I say as I turn to Blaze and look him square in the eyes, "that Blaze and I will be expecting our first cub in the next year."

The yard comes to life with yells of happiness. Blaze looks at me with fire in his eyes before leaning down and placing my middle over his shoulder. He grabs the mic from me and says, "We'll be back, maybe."

Then he ushers us back to our home. He spends the rest of the night showing me how happy he is about the news I shared.

He does wicked things to my body, stopping every once in a while, to impart words of wisdom to our cub. A few tears may have been shed during this father-child bonding time, but all it did is reinforce to me how very lucky I truly am.

EPILOGUE

BLAZE

It's been six months since we rescued everyone from the warehouse. Echo has taken his place in the Dark Leopards. He bypassed his prospect period due to his years of service in the military and because of his treatment, survival, and assistance, in rescuing the others from the ordeal they all went through. Turns out, the way they managed to nab him was that he'd had a flat tire and had pulled off to the side and was sitting in wait for help on the shoulder of the road. A tow truck showed up to assist him, he turned his back and they tranquilized him while he was looking his bike over, taking in the damage that needed to be repaired from the blown tire.

We've never been able to establish why they began taking shifters along with the humans, but Jake has been relentlessly and tirelessly questioning and interrogating those motherfuckers, Anston Greyhorse, Jason Glemson and Markus Carmichael. None have talked so far, but it's only a matter of time. Pops is being prepared to go in and ask pertinent questions to his once good buddy, Anston. Jake thinks that Anston would be more inclined to speak with Pops than anyone else.

The elders were a hard sell on the capture of our most valuable shifters; but in the end relented when they were shown all of the evidence that had been gathered and the case that had been built against them. Now, they're in a defense mode of sorts, trying to keep the council in high regards with shifters everywhere. They are a group of shifters who were voted in to protect our kind, and when it was announced that one had betrayed their oath of protection… well, let's just say all hell broke loose.

There was a frenzy that required enforcers from all branches to take off and help protect the members of the council. Their safety was in imminent, life-threatening danger; which is understandable, but also punishable by death. The only reason we agreed to send one of our own was so that an angry shifter didn't pay the ultimate penalty with his or her life. Whereas the anger is understandable, we'd have had to help in putting a shifter down, and none of us were onboard or comfortable with that nefarious idea. Especially seeing as each and every one of us could understand where their anger was coming from.

As I sit in the main room of the clubhouse, I'm surrounded by my brothers and their stories of combat and life events. A bunch of them have been over exaggerated; I know this because I was there for some of them. But this is what men do when they get together, see who's had a more adventurous life.

"Blaze," I hear my sweet mate call out my name. I'm instantly on my feet, my woman is five months pregnant with my twins. It's not uncommon for shifters to breed more than one cub at a time. We have everything super on our side; including our sperm count and egg fertilization. We do everything extra to that of our human counterparts. Our cats will always dominate our human sides, and I couldn't be any happier of a man than I am in this instance and point in our life.

"I thought you were supposed to be resting, Glory," I admonish her, but do so with a smile on my face. Happiness to lay eyes on her is overriding my need to make her do as our doctor ordered.

"I got bored. There's only so many hours in one day I can lay in that bed with my only companions being the television and my e-reader. I can just as easily rest in here with you." She bats her eyelashes at me, something she does when she's eager to get her way. It gets me every single damn time. I can't seem to resist giving her all that her heart desires. "Can't I just stay in here, Blaze?" Now, she's pulling out those sad kitty cat eyes.

"Of course, you can, as long as you actually sit and prop your feet up," I respond as her eyes light up with my acquiescence. I help her sit down and wrap my arms around her, placing my hands over her protruding belly. "Just be happy you are carrying my cubs, mate. Otherwise, I'd be putting you across my knees and spanking your bare ass for not following doctor's orders."

"Why do you insist on teasing me so, Blaze?" She pretends to sniffle, but she can't fool me with that smirk that's curling up her lips. Echo comes marching through the doors slamming them as he passes through. "Uh oh, someone's not a happy camper. Think this has something to do with that weekend trip Maritsa and her mom are going on this weekend?"

"I'd be willing to bet it has everything to do with that," I answer, feeling bad for my cousin and the fact that he can't claim his mate the way his animal is pestering him to do.

"You think he'll make it another eight months?" Glory asks me.

"I don't reckon he has much of a choice, mate." When I answer this, I forlornly watch my cousin take a bottle of tequila and head for the single men's bunkers. That's gonna be trouble I'm gonna have to keep my eyes on. I can't let him drown his sorrows away in liquor. He needs to be strong mentally and physically when the time comes for him to claim his woman.

GLORY

I've watched the last few months as Maritsa's made Echo jump through hoops for even a second of her time. But no one can disregard the way her eyes follow him if he's not glued by her side. She knows what she is to him, and boy is she making him work for it. She is determined to act her age before ultimately settling down. She's trying to experience years' worth of adventure in a few short months. She may be making him work for it, but what girl doesn't want her man to jump through hoops for her? She's young and doesn't quite grasp the concept, but she will.

Maritsa's accompanied him several times while he shifts to run at the compound. She's formed a bond with his leopard, one that she hasn't quite come to have with his human counterpart. She cares for Echo, but she struggles at times with the knowledge she has. But that's something that will happen over time, she's still in therapy and recovering mentally from her experience.

It was never revealed to those who were taken the reason behind it, they just all assume it was a human trafficking ring, one we're all complacent with them believing. In due time, Maritsa will learn the truth; and we'll all be there for her. I believe she has an inkling of why she was taken, but has never voiced that to any of us, not even Echo or Angela. She'll have tons of questions that Blaze, as well as myself, will do everything we can to explain it to where she understands.

"I hope that doesn't become an everyday thing while Maritsa's away," I say to my mate as his arms band tighter around me. Even though Angela is newly mated, she desires spending some time with just her and Maritsa before she comes of mating age. Jake isn't any more happy about their time away, but he's handling it much better than Echo is. Maybe it's because he's already marked and claimed her? I'm not sure, but it's what I suspect anyways.

"I may send him on a run. We have a pipeline that's in need of manpower. It'll be the perfect way to keep his mind occupied on something other than Maritsa." Whereas I don't know all of the ins and outs as far as the club's businesses are concerned; I do happen to know that they run illegal parts for cars throughout the United States. This is what happens when you're in another room with supreme hearing as the officers converse about club happenings. But, as a good old lady and mate, I've kept my mouth zipped firmly shut. Not even Blaze is aware that I know this about them.

"I think that'd be an excellent idea," I share with my mate.

"Then that's what I'll do." His declaration has me deflating, I hadn't realized how worried I'd been about Echo until this moment passed.

"Love you, Blaze. You're my everything."

"Love you too, Glory. My world. My love. My true mate."

And just like that, my world rights itself. I have confidence that in time, everything will work out the way it's supposed to for Maritsa and Echo. The supreme beings wouldn't have declared them as mates if it wouldn't come to pass. It's very uncommon for mates, whether shifter or human, to turn a blind eye to the gift they've been granted.

Love is in the air.

FOUR MONTHS LATER

"Push, Glory," Blaze issues as his eyes glisten with unshed tears.

"I'm pushing, I'm pushing!" I hastily declare. "I'd be more than happy to let you do this if you'd prefer."

"Honey, if that was physiologically a possibility, I'd be more than willing to take on this pain for you," Blaze declares, wiping my head with a cool cloth. Digging my nails into his wrist, I give over to my body's demands and push even harder than I was before.

"That's it, Glory. One more push and baby A will make its grand entrance into the world," Dr. Clementine, a shifter doctor, informs me. I begin to pant as I prepare myself for one more solid push. I hear a wail bouncing off the walls of this room and collapse against the bed as it's announced that we have a son.

"Delta Echo Montgomery," I announce, naming him after Blaze's father and cousin. Two men who are important to both Blaze and myself.

After pushing for another five minutes, another baby's cries can be heard. This one we're told is a girl.

"Harper Angelique Montgomery," I state; this little girl is named after both of our mothers. Two strong, loving women.

"You've given me everything a man could ever want," Blaze whispers with tears he's finally let fall free from his eyes.

"And you, my mate, have made all of my dreams come true," I reply, with tears of my own freefalling. "I thank the fates every day for making me yours."

"Best thing the fates have ever done for me, Glory. You and our two cubs complete a part of me I hadn't realized was missing."

"Ditto, Blaze. Ditto."

THE END

LIBERTY PARKER FOLLOW LINKS:

Website:
http://authorlibertyparker.com
BookBub:
https://www.bookbub.com/authors/liberty-parker
➜Newsletter sign up form: https://landing.mailerlite.com/webforms/landing/s1v0k0
➜Facebook Author Page:
https://www.facebook.com/authorlibertyparker/
➜Liberty's Luscious Ladies:
https://www.facebook.com/groups/1153797384736487/
➜Rebel Guardians Insiders:
https://www.facebook.com/groups/280929722515781/
➜Twisted Iron Groupies:
https://www.facebook.com/groups/2088172217913867/

➔Dark Leopards MC: https://www.facebook.com/groups/499498294046833/

➔Twitter: https://twitter.com/authorlparker

➔Instagram: https://www.instagram.com/libertyauthor/

ALSO BY LIBERTY

Rage Ryders MC

1. Taken By Lies

2. Taken By Rage

2.5. Taken By Vegas

3. Taken By Sadistic

4. Taken By Chaos

5. Taken By Temptation

Rage Ryders Templeton

1. Faithfully Devoted

2. Forever Yours

3. Hide & Seek

Diva's Ink

1. Blank Canvas

2. Clean Slate

3. Beautiful Template

Dreamcatchers MC

1. Charlee's Choices

2. Capturing Dreams

3. Shattered Trust

4. Utterly Wrecked

5. Blood Bond

Surrogacy

1. What Should've Been

Crossroad Soldiers MC

Prequel Walking The Crossroad

1. Our Cross To Bear

2. Claiming What's Mine

Rogue Enforcers

Maverick

Leigh

Dark Leopards MC

Blaze of Glory

Heels, Rhymes & Nursery Crimes

We All Fall Down

CO-WRITTEN SERIES

Rebel Guardians MC
(with Darlene Tallman)
1. Braxton
2. Hatchet
3. Chief
4. Smokey & Bandit
5. Law
6. Capone
7. A Twisted Kind Of Love

RGMC Box Set 1 (Books 1-3)
RGMC Box Set 2 (Books 3-7)
Rebellious Christmas (RGMC Novella) (with Darlene Tallman)

Rebel Guardians Next Generation
(with Darlene Tallman)

CO-WRITTEN SERIES

1. Talon & Claree
2. Jaxson & Ralynn
3. Maxum & Lily

New Beginnings
(with Darlene Tallman)
1. Reclaiming Maysen
2. Reviving Luca
3. Restoring Tig

Nelson Brothers
(with Darlene Tallman)
1. Seeking Our Revenge
2. Seeking Our Forever
3. Seeking Our Destiny

Nelson Brothers Ghost Team Series
(with Darlene Tallman)
1. Alpha

Rescuing Savior
(Liberty Parker with Darlene Tallman)

Twisted Iron MC
(with Kayce Kyle)
1. Mercenary And His Outlaw
2. Fueling The Edge
3. Sandman's Awakening

4. Fox's Lair
5. Pyro's Final Flame
6. Rogue's Retribution
7. Harlow's Miracle

SHARED WORLD BOOKS

Old Ladies Club
(with Kayce Kyle, Erin Osborne and Darlene Tallman)
1. Old Ladies Club - Wild Kings MC
2. The Old Ladies Club - Soul Shifterz MC
3. Old Ladies Club - Rebel Guardians MC
4. Old Ladies Club - Rage Ryders MC

Mystic Island
(with Darlene Tallman, Kayce Kyle & Hope Childs)
1. Finding The Lost

Savage Wilde:
1. Uninhibited: by Liberty Parker
2. Desire: by Darlene Tallman
3. Crave: by Kayce Kyle
4. Shameless: by Liberty Parker & Darlene Tallman… release date TBA

ANNOUNCEMENT: LIBERTY PARKER & DARLENE TALLMAN WRITING AS:

Joci Grace Morgan

1. Rise of the Raven
2. Whimsical
3. Enchantment
4. Prophecy Revealed

Printed in Great Britain
by Amazon